KARO

R. D. Torkelson

PublishAmerica
Baltimore

First printing

ISBN: 1-60610-983-9
PUBLISHED BY PUBLISHAMERICA, LLLP
www.publishamerica.com
Baltimore

Printed in the United States of America

KARO

Prologue

"Dog pile!" came the shout. Immediately the ten-year old boys sprang into action. The largest of the five was the target of the other four as they hurriedly chased after him. He was not able to escape as two of his friends leaped onto his back and the trio fell onto the grass. The other two were only a step behind and threw themselves on the top of the pile. Screams of laughter erupted from all five as they alternately rolled off and jumped back on.

The lone boy on the bottom tried to gain his feet but was thumped repeatedly back down. "You missed!" they called each time they dove on top. "You missed!" Eventually, he gave up the struggle. He knew what he had to do. It was better to say it sooner than later. "I have barf-breath," he shouted from the bottom. "Let me up! I have barf-breath," he repeated.

Hearing the magic words, the other four never rose to their feet, but rather rolled off the pile to a spot free from the melee. Within seconds, they were all lying on the ground laughing. The summer evening covered them with faint rays of red light. All five were on the grass looking up at the growing number of stars beginning to show themselves.

It was a summer ritual for these five. In the evening they would go to the Karo stadium and take turns kicking the football through the goal posts. If the kicker missed the attempt he was rewarded with a dog pile, and would have to admit, out loud, that he had barf-breath. Then, according to the rules, he would be let free and the next player would attempt his kick.

This summer evening was almost over. The light needed to see was quickly fading, and they all knew that each would be expected home soon after dark. They lay quietly on the forty-yard line looking at the waxing gibbous on the horizon.

For a long time, nobody spoke. The evening enveloped them like a warm blanket. They could have closed their eyes and slept in comfort.

"I can't wait until high school," one of them said. "We're going to have the best class Karo High School has ever seen, and we're going to win more games than any team in school history."

"We're going to kick butt," someone added quickly.

The silence returned and for another long moment the five lay motionless.

"Do you think we'll ever get out of Karo?" one of them asked.

"I'm going to go to a big city," came an answer. "I'm going to live in a sky scraper and have a million dollars."

"I'm going to be a pilot," another offered. "I'm going to fly all over the world and have a home in Europe."

There was another period of silence. "I think I'll stay in Karo," said another. "I'm going to farm a thousand acres and be my own boss."

Someone threw a handful of grass on his neighbors face. The retaliation was swift as handfuls of grass began flying through the air. Soon all five were shredding the turf and hurling dark, harmless clumps at each other. One of them picked up the ball and ran toward the end zone.

"One more time!" he shouted. "It's my turn to kick. One more time" he shouted again as he put the football on the kicking tee.

The others quickly dropped their non-lethal weapons and followed his lead to line up on the twenty yard line.

"One more time, barf-breath," came the reply

⁂

The mural at the end of the hall always caught his eye. As usual, he debated with himself whether it hade been painted by Eric Lever or Jason Hill. Both of them would have graduated about ten years ago. If he remembered correctly, Jason had gone into the Navy and had made a career of it, while Eric had been lucky enough to have an uncle working at Boeing at the time, and went right into the third shift as a parts distributor. By now, if he hadn't done anything stupid like cuss out his boss, Eric was probably making twice the salary of the man looking at the mural.

"Soar with the Eagles," the mural commanded from atop the doorway. The eagle flying over the pastel blue clouds looked down defiantly on those who passed under him. "Eric of Jason?" the man wondered as he opened the double doors to the main office. Perhaps the artist looked at that mural as his legacy to the school. Right now, somewhere on an aircraft carrier in the Indian Ocean, or sipping coffee in the union break room, one of those two could be recalling how he had worked for a semester of art class to paint it. Maybe he was bragging that it still hung over the doorway to the office. One day Eric or Jason would come back and he would ask.

Leonard Davis caught himself wondering how may years he had been in Karo. Was it twenty-five? Thirty? God, had it been that long? His first job out of college had been at a large school in Wichita. It wasn't for him.

He remembered two thousand students, 100 rooms, five administrators, four counselors and parking for 500. Every day the sheer numbers wore him down. During the first year he quickly learned he couldn't be part of such an educational factory, where he felt his job was putting a new coat of paint on poorly built cars. Go ahead, kick the tires and admire the gloss. Just don't look under the hood.

He had to get out to a smaller town, a smaller school. He wasn't really looking for the Karo job, but a friend called him and told him about the opening. The superintendent offered him the position the day of the interview. He had never intended for Karo to become his home for most of his life. But he and his new bride, Linda, moved there, reared their daughter Elizabeth, and watched as she grew up, went through college and out into the world. Elizabeth was engaged now, living in Kansas City. A spring wedding was planned. Leonard couldn't believe that in a year or two he would more than likely be carrying the title of grandfather.

Karo had been good to him. Things that once drove him crazy; the incessant gossip, the small town politics, the petty jealousies, these were things he now accepted as a small price to pay to go to sleep at night and not worry if he forgot to lock his door. His peace of mind was more important than the fact that everyone in town knew bought a six-pack of Coors every Saturday afternoon.

He knew he would spend the rest of his life in this little town a half-hour's drive from Wichita. His fiftieth birthday was just around the corner. His thin hair and slight pouch told him he was too old to start over again. He would never be any more successful than he was right now. He would have to be happy with his older home, his ten year old car, and his place on the ladder of success. Life was simple. Life was good.

Except for Linda. She had been gone three years now. They had been married 27 years when she first showed symptoms. The doctors found the ovarian cancer after it was too late. "Just make her comfortable," they said. She didn't last three months. The first year after she died, he felt as if he were living at the bottom of the Grand Canyon in the dark. The second year he began to see some daylight. This year he could feel himself slowly going up the canyon wall. He didn't want to venture a guess how far up he had climbed. He didn't want to look. He just knew he had to climb a little every day. One day he would look around and be surprised how far he was from the bottom. At least he knew which way was up.

"I see you got most of your house painted," Leonard was awakened from his thoughts as the office doors closed behind him. Riley Stewart raised a cup of coffee in his left hand as an offering. "Want some?" he queried.

"Thanks," Leonard said as he took the Styrofoam cup.

Riley poured another. "Are you sure you want your house to look puke yellow for the next ten years?" he asked with a straight face.

"It's Goldenrod," Leonard corrected, "and it's not very politically correct of you to make fun of the chromatically challenged."

Riley shook his head in mock agreement. He filled his cup, grimaced at the taste, and stared at the container as if it were to blame for its bitter contents. "I apologize," he said still staring at the cup. "But if you were to add the right color trim," he said as he turned toward Leonard, "you could be living at a Taco Tico."

"I'll put in a drive-through," Leonard quipped.

They shared a chuckle, and even though they were alone, Riley led them into his private office, and shut the door.

"How was your summer?" he asked. "Did you get away to Kansas City to see your daughter? Did you get a chance to play some golf?"

Leonard had known Riley too long. "Okay," he said after another sip, "what's on your mind? I always know when you have something important to discuss, because you always start by beating around the bush." Leonard watched as Riley grimaced slightly.

"It's about the board meeting last night, isn't it?" Leonard asked. Riley nodded as if collecting his thoughts. The Karo rural school district board meetings had become gruesome affairs. Last year they voted to cut two teaching positions from the school, and the year before it was three. There had not been a raise for the district employees in two years. Enrollment had dropped for six straight years. It was down again this year by eleven. There was serious talk about closing the school.

"They voted to eliminate three positions," Riley said flatly, "one at the elementary building and two from our building. I just don't know where we can cut again." He took another sip and sat silently.

Leonard had come to respect this man a great deal. This was Riley's last year. He had reached the golden "85 and out" combination of age and years worked to be eligible for full retirement with the Kansas Public Employees Retirement System. Riley was hoping his last year would go smoothly, but the news from last night was not a good sign.

Leonard thought that in many ways they were alike. Riley laughed easily and had a self-effacing demeanor. He knew which battles to fight and which ones to ignore. But he would never compromise his integrity. He too could have moved up the ladder of success to a larger school, but he couldn't bring himself to leave such a comfortable life in a small town.

"Who did they decide to let go?" Leonard asked already knowing the answer. "Frownfelter and Bradley?"

Riley nodded his head and took another sip. "Those were the two without tenure," he replied. "They're both young," he continued. "They'll find another place."

"Bradley and Frownfelter," mused Leonard. He looked directly at Riley. "What will this do to our master schedule?"

Riley reached into one of the piles of paper stacked on his desk, shuffled a bit, and pulled a heavily erased grid from the middle. "Surprisingly little," he said. "Class sizes will increase," he began. "We'll have to move Hunt from P.E. to Math, and Lohmiller will take over Bradley's freshmen English, Speech and Debate classes." Riley handed the paper across the desk. "We will have to drop two electives from the language arts, and one from the fine arts," he added.

Leonard scanned the graph, finished his coffee, and grit his teeth. He couldn't tell if it was the coffee or something else that had suddenly put a bitter taste in his mouth.

"There's one more thing," Riley added. "To save money, the board eliminated all assistant coaching positions last night as well." Leonard glanced over the paper toward his friend. Riley continued. "That hurts us in football, basketball, and track. We can make up for it in basketball with a title ten coach from the community. There are dozens of fathers out there who think they are Bobby Knight. In track we will have to do without an assistant. Nobody will know the difference anyway."

Riley paused for a moment to get a read from Leonard who had returned his gaze to the grid. "The problem we have is with football," he continued. "When the board dismissed Frownfelter, and then eliminated all assistant coaching duties, we were left without any football coaches." Riley paused again looking for some reaction. There was none. Was he being too obtuse? He continued. "Normally, we would just move the assistant up, but we have no assistants. I talked to the superintendent this morning, and he agrees with me as to who would be the best candidate to take over the team."

There was another pause. Leonard shifted in his seat, dropped the master schedule to his lap and furrowed is brow. Riley could see the exact moment when Leonard achieved comprehension. His eyes widened, his mouth opened, and his breath startled.

"Riley," Leonard said quietly, "you can't mean…"

Riley took a deep breath and continued. "We need you to coach the football team, Leonard. You are the most logical choice."

Leonard searched for words. "But, Riley!" he stammered. "I haven't coached for over twenty years! I haven't been on the sidelines since my first few years in Karo!" Somehow Leonard managed to speak the words without breathing.

"But you're still the best choice," Riley answered calmly.

"What about Walker? Leonard asked.

"Walker wouldn't know a first down from a hoe-down. The guy's a band teacher for God's sake."

"And I'm a Librarian," Leonard countered. "What about Harris?" he implored.

"Harris is older than I am." Riley raised his hand as if to stop the next name from coming. He paused and looked pleadingly at his friend across the desk. "I'm in a real jam here," Riley said. "My staff has been reduced by two, and of those left, the only one with any football coaching experience is you." Riley paused again. "One season," he said as soothingly as he could. "That's all I ask." He paused again. "One season."

Leonard slumped back in his chair and closed his eyes. Riley was asking for much more than that. He was asking his friend to go into the lion's den armed with nothing but faith. He was sentencing his friend to enter the fiery furnace with Shadrak, Meshak, and Abendigo. He was sentencing him to three months at a gulag for a crime he didn't commit. He was sentencing him to lead the worst football team in the state of Kansas.

The Karo Eagles held the dubious honor of the current longest losing streak of any high school in the state. The Wichita Eagle made it perfectly clear every Saturday morning on the front page of the sports section with the graphic boxes highlighting the longest winning and losing streaks. It had been almost six years since the football team had won a game. Their losing streak was now 52 and counting. Nobody gave them any chance to win this year either. Last year they lost to the defending state champion Garden Hill Hawks by a score of 82 – 0.

"Look," Riley said softly, "nobody else can do it." He paused again. "We have to have a football coach. If you don't do it, we will have to cancel the season." Riley leaned back in his chair, turned to the official KSHSAA calendar hanging on the wall next to him, and pointed to a circled date. "Practice starts in two days," he said. "You have to start getting ready."

Neither said anything for a long, silent moment. Leonard was immersed in thought. He loved football. He loved almost everything about it, but football was a harmless passion like some have for cars or fishing. He was just getting to the point where he was comfortable with the routines in his life. He liked it better when there were no surprises. Since Linda died, he had made sure of that. Now he would be coaching again for the first time in two decades? Now he would inherit the worst assemblage of adolescent athletes in the state?

"I'll owe you one," Riley said finally.

Leonard cracked a slight smile. Riley had helped him out so many times he wasn't sure that even doing this would make them even.

"Nobody expects much," Riley added quietly. "The board, the town, the school…everyone realizes the situation you have been thrown into and nobody will blame you if things don't go well. Just ride herd for a season." Riley sighed and added a last sentence. "I just wish we didn't have to play Garden Hill."

Leonard still sat quietly. He searched desperately for a way out, but he couldn't find one. He knew Riley was right. There was nobody else. Either he did it or they would cancel the season. "Okay," he finally said, "but I feel like I'm getting ready to take a walk to the gallows."

"Understandable," Riley said as he stood and headed toward the door. "Come on," he said as he opened the door, "I'll buy you another cup of coffee."

"I thought the condemned man got a whole meal," Leonard said as he joined him at the door.

"Cutbacks," Riley quipped with a tone of sadness in his voice. "Cutbacks."

An hour later, Leonard was in his office working on a state report, finishing a board report and answering a ton of unanswered mail. Now he sat with the worst football team in the state squarely on his shoulders.

⊶ ⊷

The vanity tag on the four wheel drive, multi-purpose, all-terrain sports utility vehicle read NJYNLIF. The owners thought it was both clever and appropriate. They were indeed, enjoying their life. There were no kids to bother with, the in-laws were each on a different coast, and the market was up.

Tiffany and Christopher Edwards pulled up to the chain link gate leading around to the back of the school and simultaneously muttered under their breath. The gate was locked. They would have to get out and walk. Tiffany pulled her blond hair back and began to make a pony tail. She was a small woman both in height and weight. Her small size sometimes bothered her, but she never let on. It was better to be thought of as skinny than fat. "I've got the wrong shoes on for this," she said in an exasperated monotone.

Christopher rolled his eyes, (he made sure she didn't see him) and turned off the vehicle. "Let's just scope it out," he said. "I think we could have a very good mark up here." Christopher was thin like her, but much taller. Somewhere in his ancestry there was some Lebanese, and his short, curled hair and perpetual tan attested to that. "Let's at least see what the possibilities are," he said as he opened the door.

They got out and carefully stepped over the chain. Karo High School sat vacant this Saturday morning before the beginning of school. More often than not, it would be alive with sports or community activities. It was the life-blood of the town. Established in 1908, Karo Rural High School had been destroyed by a tornado in 1971, along with half the town. Two years later it had been rebuilt with extra reinforcement, and there had been few changes to the building since then. It was solid, spacious, and capable of serving more than double the small number of students using it.

"See what I mean?" Christopher said as he pointed to the parking lot behind the gym. "There's more than enough parking." He then turned and waved toward the building. "I bet we could pick it up for a song."

Tiffany was quickly infected with his enthusiasm. She could see the possibilities. She could smell money on the horizon.

"The suits in Wichita would be crazy not to convert," he said. He pointed again. "Twenty five classrooms, two gyms, a cafeteria, and a very large storm shelter on each end of the building."

Tiffany nodded. "You might be right," she said. "The profit margin could be enormous." She broke into a wide smile, and Christopher laughed aloud. If there was one thing they both loved, it was money, and this showed possibilities of a mega-return.

Christopher suddenly stopped laughing. "We can't let anybody know," he cautioned. "It still may fall through. But the expansion of the Wichita plant is certain, and I would bet the mortgage that this will be the place they choose."

"What about your boss?" Tiffany asked. "Do you think you could pull this one off behind his back?"

"My boss," Christopher said as he walked over to his wife, "is getting ready to retire. He won't figure anything out until years after we've spent the money." With that, he lifted Tiffany off the ground and whirled her around. She protested and giggled at the same time. "We're going to make a killing," he said after two twirls and set her down. "All we have to do is help this podunk school close and next year at this time, when the project is announced, we'll have a property that would be ready for production in six weeks. "It can't fail," he said and twirled her again.

They both were thinking the same thing. If the locals in town were not bright enough to find a way to increase enrollment and keep the school open, they certainly weren't smart enough to figure out the rest. Let the school be closed. That's why God invented buses. This school of losers in this town of losers would never be missed.

They spent another hour inspecting the property. They were almost giddy when they left. There was nothing quite as sweet as forming a winning game plan. It seemed almost too easy. Karo would suffer, but they would prosper.

The August dawn came as it always did in Kansas, glowing red with a promise of searing afternoon heat. There was no dew left on the grass, so it stood brittle and brown, hardly distinguishable from the dirt below. The wind was already gathering strength to blow away the few clouds that had dared try and form during the night. As the dawn shadows faded and the pale light began to define everything, Leonard Davis led his troops from the practice field slowly toward the school.

"Take off your shoes," he ordered when the group collected at the door. "I want everyone in Mrs. Zimmerman's room in five minutes." The team showed surprise when the new coach did not run them through drills, and instead ordered a team meeting. The opening day of practice usually consisted of several hours of intense calisthenics, running, passing, blocking and tackling drills. Then in the evening, they would do the same things over again. It was the beginning of two-a-day practices, the most dreaded part of the season.

Leonard looked over his team as they filed into Mrs. Zimmerman's room and took a seat. There were sixteen players; five seniors, four juniors, three sophomores, and four freshmen. Watching them trudge into the room, he could tell they knew who they were. They knew their legacy. They were the Karo Eagles. They were the team other schools pointed to on the schedule and quickly appointed that game as their homecoming.

The five seniors came in together. The first was Brad Hoeffen. Brad was six feet tall, thin and blond. His parents had been divorced for about a year now. His father was a doctor who lived in Wichita, but Brad lived with his mother in Karo. Brad had been named a College Board National Commended Scholar for his senior year, and he was shooting for colleges with "select admissions." He was under heavy pressure from both his parents to follow in his father's footsteps. He was expected to go to the same big name university, join the same fraternity, and become a doctor.

Despite knowing his fate, Brad preferred working with plants and animals. He occasionally daydreamed about having his own greenhouse where he could study plants and maybe do research that might discover new medicines. But above all, Brad was ready to get out of Karo. He would be willing to go anywhere and study anything to get out of his house.

Next in the room came Josh Hunter. Josh was shorter than Brad, but much stronger. Josh had a crop of thick, black hair which he let grow down to his collar. He wore it that way because it drove his dad crazy. Josh was into everything at school: Student Council president, class treasurer, office aid, three varsity sports, and always a lead in the school play. Josh had a lot to live up to. His older brother had been valedictorian of his class, homecoming king, and was currently in pre-law at Washburn University. Josh had lived under that shadow for years, and it seemed no matter what he did, or how well he did it, he could never be good enough.

Following him was a big goofy guy named Alan Burns. Alan was tall, wore short cut hair, and had feet two sizes too big for his body. Alan laughed at everything and tried to make it into a joke. He was an underachiever at school and planned to be a mechanic when he graduated. Alan always walked with his head down. His father was on disability because of a "bad back," and his mother worked part time at a nursing home. Welfare had been a way of life for generations of the Burns family. No member of his family had ever graduated from high school. Even though it was never mentioned by the members of his team, everyone knew his father had a terrible temper and was considered the town drunk.

Jason Moeller came in next to Alan. He was the only true athlete in the room. Big, strong, and quick, he had a tremendous amount of natural ability. He could easily earn a scholarship to play football at a junior college, and if he had a good season this year, there was an outside chance he could play for an upper division. Jason didn't know what he wanted to do in the future, because he didn't think he would go to college, and he had never been encouraged to excel at anything. His father showed little interest in him, and his mother was always sick. Neither parent ever came to a school event.

Greg Kent was the last in the group of seniors. Greg was a quiet, shy kid who didn't challenge limits. He didn't have a competitive bone in his body. He was a preacher's son. He always found himself torn between what his parents taught him and what the world taught him. Greg did everything he was asked. He was very polite, worked hard, and was conscientious. He was very slow to anger and tried to see the positive in everything. A year ago, his mother had been diagnosed with cancer.

Coach Davis walked to the blackboard, made a list from one to five, turned to sit on Mrs. Zimmerman's desk, and waited for the room to get quiet. "Somebody tell me the most important characteristic of a successful football player," he said quietly. "What is most important?"

"How big you are?" came a reply.

"No," answered Leonard simply and scanned the room again.

"Being a mean son of a bitch." someone offered amid chuckles.

"No," came the answer again.

There was a confused pause. "How fast you are?" someone said.

"Those are all important," Leonard said as he rose and walked to the board. "But they are also over-rated. Most of them can be compensated for. I'm interested in the one tool you can use as a football player which will give you the greatest advantage over your opponent, your most important asset. Any more guesses?" There were none.

Leonard began to write. "Intelligence," appeared in the first blank. He underlined it, returned to the desk, and sat down again. "Your brain is your most important asset. It is your greatest weapon against your opponent." There was silence in the room.

"There are over 300 rules in the game of football, and you will be expected to know all of them." He hyphenated "intelligence," and wrote "rules." He turned to the team again. "You will be the smartest football team in the state," he said as he reached to the top of the desk and held up the team playbook. "This is our playbook. You will know it so well that you will be able to improvise when things go wrong. You will be able to adjust the game plan in the middle of the game. You will be able to change strategy in the middle of the huddle, and you will be able to adapt what you are doing in the middle of the play."

Leonard paused and put down the book. "You will understand the game so well that you will be able to out-think your opponent and be able to predict your opponent's moves and therefore be several steps ahead of him." He paused again. "This will require work. It will require study, and this team will have tests. There will be tests over the rules, and there will be tests over the playbook. You will have to pass these tests every week." Leonard scanned the room. There were more than a few surprised faces staring back at him.

"Coach," a hand went up in the back row. "You mean we will have a study hall as a part of football practice?"

"It will be a very important part," Coach Davis said as he walked back to the board. "Not only will it make sure you get your homework done, it will help us with the second most important asset of a football player. Does anybody want to tell me what that might be?" He waited for a response. There was none. He turned and began to write.

"Willpower" appeared in the second space. "What do I mean by willpower?" he asked as he turned to his team.

"Never give up," Alan offered.

"That's a characteristic of willpower," Leonard answered, "but it's not a definition. Someone else?" He pointed to Josh.

Josh squirmed a little in his seat. "Being mentally tough?" he offered meekly.

"Another characteristic," Leonard answered.

"An energetic determination to use our will as a tool against our opponent," Brad said.

Leonard nodded agreement. "Using our will as a tool against our opponent. Yes," he said, "I like that. Our aim is to force our will onto him. We must break his will, we must control his will, and if we do, the contest is ours."

Leonard paused. "There is a time in every contest when the real battle is not on the line of scrimmage, but in the minds of the participants. Which team can force their will on the other? Who can hold steady and strong, and who will waver and break in their resolve?" He paused again and looked at some of the blank faces staring back at him.

"Believe it or not," he continued, "most contests are won or lost at that instant. At that single moment, when one or the other loses his will, when one or the other realizes they can not force their will on the other, at that same moment, the contest is decided."

"And how do we learn willpower?" Leonard did not stop for an answer. "Through concentration and the ability to focus. The ability to do one thing at a time, do it with our best effort, learn from it, and then forget it. Those who can focus, those who can concentrate, those are the ones who have willpower."

Josh raised his hand. "Coach," he asked in a confused voice, "how are we going to practice concentration? Are we going to do brain push-ups?"

This brought a quick ripple of laughter, and Leonard found himself joining in. "Yes," he said still laughing. "That's exactly what we are going to do. We are going to do brain push-ups, brain curls, brain presses, and brain sprints."

The laughter in the room was reduced to a smattering of confused snickers. "We can exercise our bodies," Leonard said pointing to Josh, "why can't we exercise our brains?" He walked to the corner of the room to the podium where Mrs. Zimmerman gave her sleep-inducing lectures. "How do we exercise our brain?" Leonard asked. "How do we learn to concentrate?" He pulled a box from behind the podium, took it over to the desk, cleared off a space, and set it down.

"If you want to learn to concentrate," he said as he reached into the box, "play chess." With that he lifted a chessboard complete with all the pieces from the bottom of the box and set it down in front of them. "I know of nothing on this earth that forces the brain to exercise itself more than chess. It makes you concentrate, plan ahead, and focus all at the same time." This time when he looked up he saw more than a few gaping mouths. The faces staring back at him ranged from flabbergasted to bewildered. There were a few smirks as well.

Leonard walked to the front of the desk gathering his thoughts. "To me," he said as he sat on the edge of the desk, "it's a perfect match. Football and chess. They are alike in so many ways. Football is really chess with live warriors. The team that can master this game would have a tremendous advantage." He pointed to the chessboard. "This will be a part of our football practice," he said. "With this we will train ourselves to concentrate. With that concentration we will develop willpower, and with that willpower we will bend our opponents will to ours."

The room was full of disbelieving faces, but coach didn't stop to address their confusion. "What's the third most important asset of a football player?" he asked again and went to the board. The team had given up even venturing an answer. Leonard wrote "speed" in the third space. "Of all the physical attributes of a football player, the most important is speed." He looked back at his charges. There were a few heads nodding in agreement. This was finally something they could easily understand.

"How do we work on our speed?" Leonard continued. "How do we improve the quickness of our first few steps at the beginning of each play?"

"We run," Greg said without hesitation.

"That's right," Leonard nodded. "We run. We run distances to build up our endurance. We run short sprints to increase our anaerobic ability. We run five yard dashes. We do box jumps, dot drills, and jump rope. We will be in better shape than any football team we play. We are going to be the first track team to play football."

The team was no longer surprised at anything their new coach would say. They simply sat passively waiting for the next one. "But that's okay," Leonard said pleasantly, "because our running will lead us nicely into the fourth most important characteristic." He wrote on the board as he spoke. "Strength" can not be overlooked," he said as he paused and turned to address them. "And how big you are, your "size" is the last one for the list. He wrote it on the board in the fifth slot. "It would be nice to have both size and strength, but it would be better to be small and strong than to be large and weak. We will lift everyday after practice," he concluded and put down the chalk.

Leonard sat for a silent moment on the desk. He picked up the knight from the chessboard and began twirling it between his finger and thumb. There was complete silence. He turned half-way around and pointed to the board. "Intelligence, Willpower, Speed, Strength and Size," he said. "We will practice them everyday along with blocking, tackling, throwing and catching. Any questions?"

There were none. Leonard got the feeling they were a little shell-shocked. A barrage of new information, some of it completely foreign to their way of thinking had just rained down on them. They would need some time. They just sat blankly staring back at him. Some of them, no doubt, were wondering what the hell they had gotten themselves into.

"There's one more thing," Leonard said softly. "It's something I have to address before we go out on the field." He paused searching for the right words. "In the past few years, the Karo Eagles football team has had no self-respect," he said finally. "Those teams had no pride. They were willing to accept things as they were. They accepted it as their fate to be the worst team in the state. They did not have enough self-respect to care. Self-respect can only come from within. I can not give it to you. It comes from working hard to accomplish a goal on your own. Each of you must earn it by yourself."

The silence in the room was deafening. "But," Leonard said emphatically, "that is the past. That time is over. This team will not accept the past as the present. The members of this team will work so hard and prepare so well, they will be proud of who they are when they step on the field. They will not allow themselves to give less than their best effort. They will respect themselves before, during, and after the game."

Leonard spoke more softly now. "There is no shame in losing," he said. "The shame is in the lack of effort." He looked around the room and let the statement hang in the air for a minute. "If you respect yourself, you will not allow yourself to give less than your best effort. How then could you feel disgrace in a loss? And if you don't respect yourself enough to give your best effort, how can you feel satisfied, even if you win?"

The silence now was crushing. These guys had been down so long they didn't know any other way. They didn't know anything but defeat. They were losers. They knew it and the world knew it. They had been kicked in the gut so many times they had accepted lying down. Could this simple declaration now end it? Was it really that simple?

"Coach," Josh finally broke the silence and slowly rose to his feet. "I'm a senior," he said haltingly. "I was in junior high when this streak started, and I have never won a game. I've lived through it. I've endured it," he spoke with a quiver in his voice. "It's hell when everybody makes fun of you, when everybody thinks you suck. It's bad when you don't tell people where you are from because you are ashamed." Josh paused and swallowed hard. Now the quiver in his voice ended and it became strong. "I am willing to do whatever it takes to end it. It has to end. It's killing me. I don't care if I have to play chess or backgammon or read a book a week or run a marathon. I just know it has to end." Josh stood silently for a moment and then sat back down.

A few heads nodded in agreement, but most were staring at the floor. "What a perfect metaphor of where they lived their lives," Leonard thought, "heads down, looking at the floor."

"Coach," Leonard saw one of the freshmen in the back raising his hand and pointing with the other at the knight Leonard was holding. "Yes?" Leonard asked.

"What exactly does that horsey-guy do?" This time it was coach Davis's turn for a blank, open mouthed stare which quickly became a wide smile. He was still smiling a half hour later while he was timing the team in the 40 yard dash.

⊂═⊰ ⊱═⊃

There were thirteen teachers at the morning faculty meeting, two less than last year. Riley gave a few reminders to the group about the lunch schedule, hall duty, and contract time. He then talked about the new teaching assignments, and class changes. He spent a great deal of time talking about the state assessments to be given in the spring. The state AYP was increasing this year, he reminded everybody, and the school would have to work hard to achieve the state's goal and not leave anybody behind. "Unfortunately," Riley ended his presentation, "the only place on earth where all the children are above average is Lake Woebegon." Riley finished in about half an hour. He had been in the business long enough to know that after thirty minutes, the worst students on the face of the earth were a group of teachers.

Today was the first day of school, and every school year began with fresh possibilities. Every student could make the honor roll, every teacher could be a master teacher, and every team was undefeated. The real world would set in soon enough. After several weeks much of the enthusiasm would have worn off, and some teachers would begin counting the days before Christmas.

When the first bell rang, the teachers gathered with the students in the gym. The students usually sat with their class, and the teachers stood as a group to the side. New school clothes were everywhere. They were all t-shirts and jeans, but they were new t-shirts and jeans. The students quieted when Riley gave his usual "welcome back to school" spiel peppered with rules and jokes.

Leonard found himself studying the faces in the bleachers. He knew stories behind every face. He could go down the row and recall something joyous, and unfortunately, something sad about each of them. Some of those stories should not be attached to such young faces.

What disturbed him the most was how detached many of them were. Nobody had ever connected with them. Nobody had ever reached them. He used to wonder why. He couldn't understand how some of them could feel so apathetic and isolated. How could so many seem to have no moral compass and no borderline on their behavior? But he knew the answer. They were detached because America does not love them, and they know it.

Oh, America would deny it, but the evidence was overwhelming. America does not love its children. It kills millions of them every year before they even take their first breath. It allows millions more to live in hunger and poverty. It surrounds them with sex and drowns them in drugs. It tells the boys that fathers are not important and there are no good men. It tells the girls, "you can have it all, but you must use your body." It adores possessions over people. It tells others to rear their children for them. He wanted to shout to every parent in America, "your child is your main job. Don't give your child your things, give your child your time." The sad truth was that America could solve all of those problems if it wanted. It didn't want to.

Leonard no longer wondered why so many of them were so detached. He wondered why more were not so. He always clenched his teeth when he heard a politician say something "for the children." What a farce. America doesn't love its children, and they know it.

He saw the senior girl with the older boyfriend in a possessive relationship. He wanted marriage, and she wanted to go to college and explore the world. There was the local beauty pageant winner who wanted to go to college to get away from her domineering parents and lead her own life. Talking to her was a senior girl whose father was dying from hepatitis. Thirty years of hard drinking had finally caught up with him. Their family talked every year about moving to Florida for his last days.

He saw the freshman boy who liked to shock people with his knowledge of the occult. Next to him was the freshman girl pregnant with the child of a boy who had graduated last year. She was talking to a senior boy who had a learning disability and wanted to farm for a living. He would be a good farmer. All the teachers knew this and passed him on his effort alone.

Behind him sat the pot head who did just enough work to pass. He just wanted to do his dope. His brain was slowly turning into guacamole. He was talking to the senior girl who used sex to get whatever she wanted. She was a good artist who thought everybody else was a non-creative robot.

Toward the back he saw a sophomore girl whose dad had just been diagnosed with an inoperable brain tumor. Next to her was a senior boy who was in his fifth year of high school. He would probably drop out before the end of the semester. They were talking with a junior girl whose second grade cousin drowned last year, and a sophomore girl whose parents divorced over the summer after twenty-four years of marriage.

His eyes went from face to face. Images and thoughts flashed to the front and retreated. Knee operation from a basketball injury. Single parent who comes to school two or three times a week. Quit school last year to get a job, and back for another try. Living with grandparents and hating it. Few acquaintances, no friends. Makes up stories to shock people and get attention. Mother is an alcoholic. Tired of being the perfect kid. Sexually active since fourteen. Gifted and wants you to know it. Ward of the court who had run away from home several times. Made advances to another girl in P.E. Pathological liar. Vandal. Constantly rocks back and forth when talking. Still had an invisible umbilical cord attached to his mother.

Every face had a story. For half of them, there was no father in the home. If he thought about it too much, he could easily get depressed. But they made up the student body, and he was bound to them. He had to help them on their journey. In many cases nobody else would.

The assembly was soon over, and Riley dismissed the seniors first, juniors second and so on as was the tradition. The enthusiasm of the day was contagious. The promise of youth always made Leonard optimistic. Working with teenagers would either keep you young or kill you.

Leonard followed the herd back through the hall as they dispersed into their various classrooms. He went in the office for a cup of coffee. He was surprised to find himself excited about the new school year, and he was even anticipating the upcoming football season. Could it be that he might enjoy coaching again?

"I hear you decided to take over the macho playground." Leonard looked up from filling his cup to see Martha Stapleton stirring creamer into her "save the planet" cup. What a way to begin the day. He didn't want to engage in a verbal joust with the queen of the acid tongue.

"Morning Martha," Leonard nodded as he took his first sip.

"I prefer Ms. Stapelton," she replied with a half smile. "Tell me something," she continued to talk through the smile, "you're somewhat intelligent for a man, so why you would want to ride a dying horse? What could possess you to take over the football team?"

"That's a sad image for an animal lover," Leonard said and reached for the artificial creamer himself. She was in true form this morning, he thought.

She rolled her eyes slightly and pretended to ignore his comment. "After all," she continued, "it's just a matter of time before that brutal sport is dropped. And if we wanted to save money, this would have been a perfect time."

Leonard looked around the office to see if anyone else was in. No help on the horizon. He was on his own. "And why do you say that?" Leonard regretted asking the question the second it left his lips.

Martha furrowed her brow. "Because this school is dying and we had a perfect chance to save some money by dropping that barbaric ritual of male bonding disguised as sport. But then you had to come along on your white horse and save the day."

"What's with the horses?" Leonard thought. "The money crunch isn't as bad as people think," he answered trying to sound convincing. "Enrollment is only down about a dozen. We'll get through this."

Her famous half-smile returned. "A sinking ship," she said simply. "The Karo school district has holes in it the size of a truck. It's not a matter of if this school closes; it's a matter of when. You can live in your dream world, but I, for one, will not go down with the ship." She took another sip.

"I'm sure you have a lifeboat somewhere within your reach," Leonard said.

"I'm very close to completing my degree in administration," she told him. Leonard didn't think there was a member of the faculty who had not been given that sentence at least a half-dozen times last year. "And when I've got that degree, then I'm on the train out of here and the good old boys had better watch out."

"Because you're going to mix metaphors?" Leonard couldn't help himself.

"You're attempts at humor don't change the facts," she returned to her half-smile, "and the facts are there is a better than reasonable chance this will be the last year for this school, and you taking on the football team was just a waste of money that could have gone to help in important ways."

Leonard had played defense long enough. "Look," he said as dispassionately as possible, "this is not some Hollywood movie where you say something clever to put me in my place and I stand speechless. This is the real world. And in the real world, one can either help or get out of the way. Yes, we may very well lose the school, but let's go out fighting to save it." Leonard turned to head out of the office, but turned again before he left.

"The easiest thing in the world to do is criticize. Let's try something hard. Let's try and make things better." Leonard didn't wait to hear a response. He left the office and walked down the hall. He suddenly felt the urge to visit some classes and see some of the great kids sitting in the desks.

The August sun beat mercilessly on the practice field. Coach Davis could see waves of heat flowing up from the ground, distorting the view of everything on the horizon. It was break time, and the team sat around the water hose taking turns drinking and splashing water over themselves. Some turned their helmets upside down, filled them with water, and amid laughs from those watching, put the helmet back on causing a deluge that soaked them from head to foot.

This is good, Leonard thought to himself. The guys were enjoying themselves. They were working hard, and they were having fun. In fact, Leonard had been pleasantly surprised by what he had seen. His line was small, but they were solid. His ends were not very fast, but they could catch the ball. The backfield lacked quickness, but they were able to follow the blocking patterns. There were no surprises though, because with the exception of his standout athlete Jason, he had an average team with average talent.

At quarterback, Brad Hoeffen did not have an arm to throw the ball very deep, nor the speed to outrun many people, but he had almost mastered the playbook in the first week. Brad showed great insight, and that might make the difference in a game or two.

"Who'd you kill to get this sentence?" Leonard turned around to see William Roundtree pointing out toward the team.

"Nobody," Leonard answered. "I've spent too much time alone with the boss's wife."

"Well," came the quick response, "I've seen that woman. You've been punished enough."

The two greeted each other with a handshake, and shared a quick laugh. "How are you doing, William?" Leonard asked. "Are you ready for another year?"

"The fun's just starting," William gave his standard reply, and it brought a smile to Leonard. No matter how many times he heard his friend say it, it always brought a smile. William Roundtree was one of his favorite people in the world. William always had a good word for you, or if he thought you needed it, a swift kick in the pants. Since Linda died, their friendship had become even more important. Leonard had a standing invitation for Sunday dinner at the Roundtree home. He rarely missed the opportunity.

William was full blooded Cherokee. His shoulder length, black hair was tinted with occasional gray and kept in a pony tail at all times. In order to get off the reservation, he joined the Marines the week after he graduated from high school in Oklahoma. After six months of training, William found himself sleeping in the jungles of Vietnam and trying to stay alive. He spent two years in country as a grunt.

It was not a smooth transition from the world of war to the world of peace for William. He accepted a football scholarship at Wichita State University with the intention of studying business. But his college days quickly became a series of confused memories about getting drunk and waking up in strange places. He lost his scholarship the first year and his place at the university the second. If he had not met Samantha, he would more than likely be dead by now.

William was the supervisor of all maintenance for the district. If a bus needed repair, he fixed it. If the boiler broke over the weekend, he fixed it. If a room needed to be re-wired for a new air conditioner, William did it. He did everything from drive a bus route to fix leaking toilets.

It had taken Leonard a while to get to know William. He was a hard man to get to know. Even though life has a way of chipping away walls, there were some things not even decades of erosion could change. Sometimes in his dreams, William would hear mortars. He would hear Hueys. He would be sleeping in the rain. He would wake up in a sweat.

Leonard never brought it up because William refused to talk about it. Maybe some things were just best left buried.

"My biggest problem is numbers," Leonard said waving at the team members who were still taking every opportunity to soak themselves. "I only have sixteen players. We can't even scrimmage."

"I can see that," William nodded. "Maybe some more will come out?"

"No," Leonard said. "I don't believe any more of the good young men of Karo will choose to join us. I just need some way to show alignments, positions, blocking schemes and such. It's one thing to put them on a blackboard, but then I come out here and say "imagine there's a linebacker here," or "imagine the defensive tackle takes this position." Leonard shook his head again.

"I wish I could do something about that," William said.

Leonard appreciated the thought. He knew it was sincere. "Well, there's nothing that can be done," he said, "unless you can increase the population of Karo for me." Leonard hesitated after that comment, hoping William would not take his joke the wrong way. William or Samantha, Leonard never learned which one, was unable to have children. They had been childless for their twenty six year marriage.

They both stood silently for a moment, and then William turned to go. "Let me think about it for a while. But right now I have to get the buses ready for the state inspection." William was clearly agitated. "With all I have to do to get ready for the beginning of the year, those yahoos at the state called me yesterday afternoon and said "Oh, by the way, the highway patrol will by in town tomorrow for inspection."

Leonard tried not to laugh, but he did anyway. "Welcome to the new year," he said. "The fun's just starting."

William smiled back. "See you Sunday," he said as he walked away.

“Hello Leonard.”

Leonard looked up from his table and smiled. He recognized the voice. “Hello Elaine,” he answered. He gazed for a moment in silence. He wanted to say something about how wonderful she looked, but chose not to. “Are you ready for a new school year?” he asked. That was a safe question.

“Oh I suppose so,” Elaine answered. “The summers always go so fast. I don’t get half the things done I want to.”

“I know the feeling,” Leonard said as he nodded in agreement. He dropped his pen to the table and walked over to her. Elaine Simmons was the school psychologist for the district. Actually, that was misleading because she traveled to five different schools as part of her job. These five small towns were within an hour’s drive of each other. No one school could afford her services alone, but through the county co-op, each could afford to pay the twenty percent required for her salary. In return, she rotated from school to school one day a week during the year. Karo saw her on Wednesdays.

Leonard had dealt with Elaine as a member of the Student Improvement Team for the last two years. He had to work with a committee of teachers to make sure any pre-assessment on a student who might have special needs was finished before referring him or her to Elaine for testing.

"Good to see you," Leonard said. "You look well." Leonard bit his lower lip. Could that have been more lame? You look well? Was he her doctor? Maybe he was pretending to be a favorite uncle who always greeted her with "you look well, Elaine. Here's a quarter." Oh well, it didn't matter anyway. He was getting way to ahead of himself. Even if he were interested, he was out of the picture. He couldn't get involved again so soon. It hadn't been long enough. Besides, rumor had it that she already had a steady boyfriend. Some lawyer in Wichita.

But Leonard couldn't keep his eyes off her. She kept her short brunette hair curled just the right way around her ears. He loved the occasional flash of a gray strand he sometimes caught sight of. Her skin was smooth and her eyes sparkled when she laughed. He really enjoyed her laugh. She was easy to look at, and easy to remember. Yes, Leonard thought to himself, she was a handsome woman. Handsome? Leonard bit his lip again. As the kids would say, "get a clue."

"Thank you," Elaine replied with a sincere smile. "You look well too." For an instant, Leonard thought he saw something in her eyes, a spark, a smile, an invitation. But he must have been imagining things. He had been out of circulation for so long he couldn't read things like that anymore. There was no sense in playing these games anyway. Nobody could ever replace Linda. He didn't even try to think otherwise. He had been content these past few years with his routines. He could go the rest of his life with them. Besides, someone like Elaine was out of his league.

"Please," Leonard motioned toward a chair, "have a seat."

"No, thanks," she declined. "I have to go to the grade school building for a staffing. I'm running late as it is. I just thought I would stop in and say hello. See if you were ready for the new year. That sort of thing."

"I'm glad you did," Leonard said trying not to sound disappointed.

"We'll see each other next week," Elaine said. "We have an IEP meeting for Caleb Wilson."

Leonard searched his memory for a second. "Right," he suddenly remembered. "The new sixth-grader from Wichita. Yes. Sure. I'll get with Riley and have him fill me in on the when and where."

"Okay," Elaine said as she nodded her approval. She smiled at him again. There was an awkward silence. "Well," she slowly reached to the floor for her briefcase. "See you next week." She paused, and then turned around.

"Next week then," Leonard called out as she walked out of the office. He slowly walked back to the table and sat down. He picked up the state assessment data and resumed his work, but his head wouldn't follow. Had he seen something in her eyes? Did she hesitate to leave?

What was he thinking? He was fooling himself. He should stop this nonsense right now. He had his chance at love and it was over. He would spend the rest of his life alone. He wasn't interested. He would just have to make do the best he could.

An eye began to tear. He missed Linda so much. He missed 23 years of companionship. Now he understood why some primitive cultures would inflict physical pain on themselves, perhaps cut off a finger, when a close one died. It gave them something physical they could relate to. It made it easier to deal with an emotional pain that never left. The pain came less often, but it never went away.

Leonard wiped his eye. No. It would never happen. He couldn't start dreaming that someone like Elaine would ever be interested in someone like him. He was way past his prime. He would have to accept a solitary life. He would have to find comfort in his routines. He had his shot. Love rarely blesses one man twice in a lifetime.

He picked up the assessment results again, and fortified that his fate was set, was able to concentrate. Still, occasionally, he would remember her smile and wonder if he had seen something in her eyes.

Alan pulled the old gray pick-up into the dirt drive, saw that his mom's car was gone, and shuddered. She would be working late at the nursing home. His dad would be home alone. The routine between mom and dad was very predictable. Every Thursday after she got paid, she would cash her check and bring home the bottle as ordered. Then she would keep out of the way until after dinner. Most of the time she ended up putting Alan's father to bed before dark.

The problem was that sometimes she had to work a double shift and would not be around when Alan got home. Alan parked the truck next to the faded red barn with the missing front door. A couple of old dogs came trotting out of the barn, barking loudly until they recognized the driver. A group of cats scattered under his feet when he stepped out of the truck. He gently moved them away and walked toward the back door of the old farmhouse.

The old house badly needed painting. Scattered around the yard were several old cars and trucks sitting on cement blocks. There had been numerous promises to fix them. There had been promises some day to fix the boarded windows, promises to throw away the piles of trash filling the backyard, and promises to fix the barn. There had been so many promises. For as long as Alan could remember there had been promises. He paid no attention to them now. Now they made him laugh.

Maybe his dad would be asleep. Most of the time when he hit the bottle, he would just mumble to himself and sleep it off. But sometimes he would get mean and do stuff to him or mom that he could never tell anyone. Most of the time, however, his mom would cower in the background, wring her hands and look at the floor.

Alan didn't know which parent he despised more, his father for being such a mean drunk, or his mother for being so weak. The night Alan was in the fourth grade and forgot to feed the dogs, his dad chained him with them for the evening. He always remembered his mother looking out the window from time to time with such a sad, hurt face, pretending she couldn't do anything about it, and his dad with an occasional loud bark outside the back door.

At least now that Alan was bigger, the beatings had just about stopped. His dad knew that his days of dominance were coming to an end, and he couldn't remain the strongest forever. He knew the day was coming when Alan would have the upper hand. At times Alan even hoped his dad would start something, so he could finish it. He would outlast him. He would outlast him and finish it.

The door swung open just as Alan pulled on the screen door. His dad appeared, unshaven in the same T-shirt and jeans he had worn for two days. Bottle in hand, the smell of Jack Daniels surrounded him.

"Where the hell you been, boy?" The bottle tipped to its target.

"I had football practice," Alan said as he tried to enter the house. His way was blocked.

"Football practice!" The voice was rough and angry. "What the hell you wastin your time with football practice when there's chores to do?"

"I'm on the team," Alan stepped back. His eyes were straight ahead so he wouldn't look directly at his father. "I got to practice if I want to play."

There was another swig on the bottle and another angry retort. "I don't give a good God damn about your damn football team. Them chores ain't going to do themselves."

"I'll do them when I get home," Alan said and tried again to enter the house. The bottle suddenly appeared in Alan's chest pushing him backwards. His dad backed him all the way off the porch and into the yard.

"You think you're too damn good to do chores around here? Is that it?" Alan saw the aluminum bat hiding in his dad's left hand. "Well let me tell you, you ain't nothing but a bag of shit, and you ain't ever going to amount to nothing more than a bag of shit."

The bottle found its target again.

"I'll do the goddamn chores," Alan shouted.

"I'll tell what else you're going to do," his father shouted. "You're going to quit that bunch of loser assholes you call a football team." The bat came out from behind him and smashed against the side of the porch rattling the door and windows. "I want the goddamn chores done before the sun sets."

"I don't want to quit the team," Alan stood his ground. "I don't care if we lose all our games. I like playing. I like the guys on the team, and I like the coach."

The bat smashed the side of the porch again. "You think those panty-waist sons of bitches care about you? You think they care about a "Burns?" Ain't nobody give a shit about the "Burns" family around here for years. What makes you think you're so goddamn special? You ain't better than me." The bottle took another trip to its owner's mouth.

"I'll do the chores when I get home from practice," Alan said through clenched teeth.

"You'll do as you're goddamn told." This time the bat was raised. Alan stepped back. "You'll quit that sorry excuse for a team and you'll get home after school, and you'll do your damn chores."

For an instant Alan considered resistance. Why not? Why not just rush the son of a bitch? Either his father would hit his mark or miss. One way he would live, and the other way he would die. What did it matter? Living like this could not be better than death.

His dad could sense it too, and during that same instant, old man Burns couldn't tell if he would have to swing to kill.

Alan backed away, swallowed hard, turned around, and headed toward the barn. "I'll do the goddamn chores," he said.

The bottle found its mark again. There was hate in those eyes this time as he watched his son walk away. "You think you're better than me?" he called out. "You hear me?" he shouted even louder. "You ain't no better you lazy sack of shit." He took another drink and walked back into the house kicking and cussing at the cats all the way.

“Everybody over here!” Leonard called to the team. The water break ended and his charges gathered around. “Take a knee,” Leonard said and waited until everyone was silent.

“We have an hour before we go into the classroom,” he began, “and I still want to go through some more drills. But before that, I want to let you know that we’re going to do the statistics a little differently this year. There will be no individual statistics reported until after the season is over.”

There was no reaction from the team. Maybe they had come to expect the unexpected. “We will keep statistics for the team’s total, but there won’t be any individual numbers on how many yards one player gained or how many tackles another player had. It’s just going to be a team total. After we’ve finished our last game, then we will look at how each individual did during the season.”

Leonard took his hat off and rubbed the brim. He waited for a reaction. “Why are you doing that, coach?” Jason asked.

“Because no individual should be placed above the team,” Leonard answered. “To me a team is something that has its own identity; it’s something in which the sum truly becomes greater than its parts.”

Leonard looked around at some confused faces. “Look,” he said, “the Marines have a code that explains it all pretty well. A team is a lot like a machine. It doesn’t whine or complain when it is working hard because working hard is what it is supposed to do. A successful team will always look out for the good of the group before the good of the individual. A team will not sacrifice long term goals for a short term satisfaction. A successful team will always do its very best job no matter how easy or difficult the task, and a successful team does not choose the easy wrong over the difficult right. Members of a successful team trust each other because they do not lie to each other. And finally, a successful team will only judge its members by their words and actions. Everything else is just window-dressing."

Nobody raised a hand, but Leonard felt compelled to continue. "Look," he said putting his hat back on, "somebody tell me which is more important to my car, the gas tank or the steering wheel? Could I use the car without either? Which is more important, the tires or the engine? I believe if a team is a machine, then all parts are equally important. If one part is missing or does a bad job, then the whole car suffers. If one spark plug is not performing, then my entire car will run poorly."

"Coach," Brad interjected, "you're lucky if your car runs downhill."

There was a quick burst of laughter, and Leonard found himself laughing too. He hoped he was explaining himself well enough. "I want us to be like that car. "And you know" he started again, "when every part of our machine works together, why, it's one of the most beautiful things in the world. And that's what I want from us. I want each of us to do his part. A tire can't do the job of a carburetor, and spark plug can't do what a windshield does, but if everyone does his part, the machine will run like it should."

"Then," Leonard continued, "the question becomes, what do we do when things go wrong? Like any machine, things sometimes break down. What do we do if our car has a flat tire? Do we get out and cuss the tire? Maybe. But what good does that do? The tire is still flat."

"We change the tire," Greg said.

"Yes," Leonard answered. "It's as simple as that."

The team was silent. "During every game," Leonard began softly, "we're going to have things go wrong. Somebody will fumble. There will be an interception. There will be a penalty, or the refs will make a bad call. How we react to those bad things is just as important as how we play the game. And I asked myself over and over how we could prepare for when things go wrong. What I've come up with is called, appropriately, the "flat tire" drill."

Instantly, there were many confused, worried faces. They had come to know that when coach had new ideas, they could count on something unusual. What would it be this time?

"We are going to prepare for bad things," Leonard continued, "by experiencing them. We are not going to complain or blame each other when we have a "flat tire." We will accept it. Then, when we get in a game and something bad happens to us, we will accept it, address the problem, fix it, learn from it, and forget it. Life is full of flat tires. Why should this football team be any different?"

He looked around anticipating questions, but there were none. Most of them were nodding their heads slightly. He was not telling them anything they did not already know.

"We are not going to lose heart when bad things happen," Leonard began again. "We are going to remain a team. We will win as a team and we will lose as a team. Any praise or blame will be shared equally by every member of the team."

There was a brief silence.

"What's a "flat tire" drill," Josh asked as if he really didn't want to know.

"At random times throughout practice," Leonard said measuredly, "I will call out "flat tire!" Immediately everyone will stop what he is doing, run to the track and take one lap around it. Then when everyone returns, we will resume our practice as before. You will not be able to predict when a "flat tire" will occur during practice because you will not be able to predict them during the game. We must condition ourselves to handle the random, discouraging affects of bad things, and this is what I've come up with."

Leonard looked at the silent faces around him. Bad things were not new to them. They had experienced enough of them throughout their years. They had learned how to quit, and they had learned how to accept losing. They had learned blame, and they had learned to take the easy path.

"FLAT TIRE!" Leonard shouted. Some of them looked up as if they had been asleep. Brad and Josh immediately grabbed their helmets and began running toward the track. The others quickly followed. A few moaned aloud as they looked at their crazy coach, picked up their helmets and turned to catch the others.

"Why does random have to be now?" Leonard heard as they left.

Jason picked up the keys from the table and walked quietly down the hall. He made as little noise as possible. His father sat in his recliner, newspaper in his lap, mouth open, television on, and eyes closed. Seeing his dad napping as he was, Jason knew it was Wednesday.

He knew it was Wednesday because on Monday nights there was a standing penny-ante poker game at Charles Blake's house. Charles, being a bachelor, looked forward to hosting the weekly binge of beer, bad jokes, belches and bitching. Tuesday and Thursday nights were bowling nights in Warfield. Friday was T.G.I.F. with the guys after work. On the weekends, if he couldn't play golf, he would watch whatever sport was on T.V. at the time.

That left Wednesday night as the night for Dennis Moeller to embrace his family. Sometimes, as was the case now, he would embrace them while sleeping in his chair. But usually, he would spend his quality time chuckling occasionally with the laugh track of whatever mindless sitcom he was watching. Every other now and then, he would be supportive by drinking a few too many beers and going off early to bed.

As much as Jason despised his father's routine, he couldn't bring himself to condemn it. He could almost understand it. Jason looked at him lying there with his mouth open. In a few minutes, the snores would come. He looked, but could not condemn.

"Is that you dear?" Jason heard a weak call from the bedroom. He hesitated for a moment, deciding if he could continue walking and not be detected. Years of trying told him he could not.

"Jason?" came the call again. "Is that you?"

"Yeah, mom," Jason answered through the door trying not to sound frustrated. "What do you want?"

"Come in for a minute,"

Jason squinted when he entered the darkened room. "I was just going out. I was going over to Nikki's house. We have a geometry test tomorrow and I thought we could study together."

"Come in for a minute."

Jason opened the door and through the pale light he saw his mother in her housecoat sitting up in bed. He looked at her pale skin and weary eyes. She was a victim of life. Life was suffering. Life was cruel. Life was hard, and she was going to prove it. She spent most of her time in bed or puttering slowly around the house. The busier her husband got, the sicker she became. The sicker she was, the busier he became. When she occasionally left the house, it was to make sure people in town knew how much suffering she was enduring.

"Oh no," she said as Jason entered the room. "That won't do," she spoke in a pitiful voice. "I need you to stay home tonight. Your father is busy, and I would feel better if you were around in case I needed you."

Jason didn't say anything. He would only make her feel worse if he wasn't careful. He came over to the bed and sat on the edge. "I have some good news," Jason said with real enthusiasm. "I got a recruiting letter today. It's the first letter I've gotten about playing football at college. Coach says I will probably get more as the season goes along." He stopped short when he caught his mother's eye.

"I'm not feeling very strong these days," she began. "I think you should stay at home and go to the local junior college. Your father is too busy, and I need someone around, at least until I get my strength back."

"But, mom," Jason protested. "The junior college in this county doesn't even have football! Coach says I might have a chance for a scholarship. Opportunities like that don't come along for everyone."

"It will just be until I get my strength back," his mother reached out and took his hand. "Please don't abandon me. I would never abandon you. My mother died when I was…."

Jason pulled his arm back and stood up. This time he could not hide his frustration. "I know! I know! Your mother died when you were just seven years old. I've heard it a thousand times." As soon as he finished saying it, he regretted it. Tears began to form in his mother's eyes. She reached for him with both hands this time.

"Please don't be mean to me," she implored. "I do so much for you. All I ask is for some support. Is that too much to ask?"

Jason sat back down on the bed and took his mother's hand in his. He didn't look at her. If he did he would become angry again. In the background he could hear a television commercial about indigestion interrupted by an occasional sound which could only have been a snore.

"Can't you see?" Jason finally looked at his mother. "This may be my only chance. I'm not really good at very many things, but coach says I am very good at football. And I could get a college education paid for by playing on the team. If I don't accept, my chances of ever playing again will be gone."

"It will just be until I get my strength back," she said weakly. It was as if she hadn't heard a word Jason had said. "I'm only asking for a few years. Is that too much for a mother to ask?"

Jason looked up at the ceiling and closed his eyes. He could hear his mother begin to cry quietly. He reached over for a tissue and handed it to her. He continued to hold her hand as she wept. He noticed his jaw was so tight, it was hurting.

"You go off to your friend's house," his mother said through her tears. "I think I will be okay. If I need something, maybe your father can get it. You go on and study with your friend." She began to dry her eyes and put on the face of a martyr. She straightened herself, picked up her magazine, and began to read. "Don't worry about me," she finally said. "You go on ahead. I'll be fine."

Jason found himself walking past the sleeping figure in the recliner and was quickly out the front door into the cool of the evening. He probably wasn't good enough to get a football scholarship. Maybe junior college wouldn't be so bad.

One could walk into the Karo city park and not be able to distinguish it from a hundred others in the state. There were two swings set in the shade, a merry-go-round on the other side of the trees, a jungle gym, and a giant slide. Right next to the shelter, the restrooms were open air and would occasionally back up. On the other side of the park, stood a tennis court with a basketball goal at the top of the backstop. One had to choose, tennis or basketball.

An old red caboose, which had been given to the city by the Atchison, Topeka, and Santa Fe Railroad back in 1978, sat next to the water tower. It showed signs of age with its peeling red paint, broken windows, and sagging railings. One Halloween about ten years ago, some pranksters tried to start a fire in it. Nothing burned. The fire did, however, leave a permanent smoky smell on the inside.

With just a small variation on this theme, every small town in Kansas had the same park. But it was well kept and still popular with young and old alike. The young would come for a pick-up basketball game or to hang out. The old would sit in the shade and talk about how good things were in times past.

Christopher and Tiffany Edwards leaned forward on the uncomfortable cement bench, their elbows coming to rest on the uncomfortable cement picnic table. Across the table sat Edgar Fortus. Edgar weighed 360 pounds. Edgar did not believe in deodorants, rather he still believed in the traditional bath once a week on Saturday Evening. Edgar was single.

Edgar didn't move around very well these days. If he sat in any chair but the one he had at home, it would take him several minutes to get himself out. He always had a three day beard that rolled around his double chin when he spoke. Edgar began almost every sentence with "is."

Edgar was pondering. "Is…let me ponder on that," he liked to say. Edgar was one of the seven citizens of Karo who held a position on the local school board. He had been elected on two issues. He wanted to keep taxes down, and he wanted to keep those "Wichita people" out. He had been very successful with both. The town was going broke, and the school was dying.

Tiffany and Christopher hated doing business with Edgar, but they had no other choice. He was the only member of the board they felt they could approach with their plan. They were not surprised when Edgar had shown interest. But this was, at best, a strained partnership.

"It's a simple matter," Christopher said in his calmest voice. "We need someone on the board to make the proposal and push it through."

Edgar took off his straw hat and rubbed his brow. The red lines on his forehead looked like permanent scars. Edgar's farm was not doing well. He had too many bills. He was just hanging on year to year. Prices were down and there had not been enough moisture last winter for this year's crop to grow properly. And cattle prices! Don't get him started.

"Is…let me get this straight," Edgar said. "You want me to propose the board close the school?"

"There's $50,000 in it for you if you can get it to pass," Christopher said again with his calmest voice.

"$50,000 tax free money," Tiffany added.

Edgar usually put on the affect of a simple minded fella, but underneath he knew how things were done. He knew a scam when he heard it. Something told him he would like this. Tiffany and Christopher knew this too. This simple acting farmer was as sharp as a tack when it came to money. Edgar had been part of several questionable business ventures and even bragged about how he always outsmarted Uncle Sam when April 15 came around.

"Is…what have you got in mind?" he said sternly. "And don't give me politician speak. I don't want as little of the truth as possible as slowly as possible."

"Here's the plan," Tiffany took a quick glance at her husband. She could tell he was losing patience. They would have to end the negotiations soon. She turned to Edgar and talked as if she were explaining the coefficient of friction to a sixth grader. "If we can get the school to close, the useless building will remain empty, collecting dust. Then after a few months, people will be pleased when we buy it from the district for what will seem a fair price."

"Is…why would you want to do that?"

"We would be in a position to turn it over for a substantial profit," Christopher answered.

"Is…how substantial?" Edgar hated both of them simply because of who they were and how they were acting right now. They were arrogant, condescending assholes who put a slice of lemon in their beer. He knew they thought of him as a red-neck buffoon. Each eyed the other with hidden contempt. But each knew they would have to put up with each other for the chance to make money.

"Enough to give you $50,000 cash," Christopher said trying not to show his anger.

"What the hell's the hurry?" Edgar asked. "Is…the school's gonna close in a year or two anyway."

"Our window for that substantial profit will only be open for a short period of time," Chris answered. He found it harder to control his anger. "So, the school must close this year."

"Is…why do you need me?" Now Edgar was being purposely dense.

"Neither of us is on the board," Tiffany said to her imagined sixth grader, "so neither of us can propose the consolidation."

"Is…why don't I just buy the building myself?" Edgar asked.

Chris had to turn away or he would call that 360 pound ameba something offensive and the negotiations would be over. For his part, Edgar grinned inwardly. He had gotten to one of them.

"Because you would draw suspicion." Tiffany answered. "People would talk. If you did it there might be an investigation. The best way to do this is to divide everything into three seemingly unrelated parts, with two unrelated partners, followed by a completely unrelated chain of events. No one will ever know as long as there is plausible deniability. You win. We win."

"Is...let me ponder it a while," Edgar said as he put his hat back on. He looked down towards the ground. "I sure could use the extra money," he spoke as if he were alone. He looked up. "Especially if Uncle Sam don't ever hear about it."

"Nobody will ever know," Christopher said calmly.

Edgar gave the signal that the conversation was over when he began to pull his legs out from under the cement picnic table. He had to use both hands to do it, and he had to do it one leg at a time. He sat for a moment rubbing his knees. They always gave him trouble.

"Is...I want half the money now," Edgar stated this as if it were non-negotiable.

Tiffany and Christopher said nothing, because they were not completely surprised. In fact, they had discussed such a development, and in the end, decided it would be a good thing. It would marry him to the plan so he couldn't back out. "You will receive a large envelope in the mail," Christopher said with as little emotion as possible. "After the board votes and the school is officially closed, you will receive another large envelope. But it must be done before Christmas. Preferably before Thanksgiving."

"Is...I'll be expecting a special delivery," Edgar said as he stood to walk to his pick-up truck. "It's a half-assed plan," he said as he turned to go, "but it might just work."

Tiffany and Christopher sat silently until Edgar was in his car and out of earshot. They even waited until he had driven completely out of the park before they began to curse and swear about the indignity of dealing with that stupid, fat, bastard. But, they reminded themselves as they stepped into their SUV, it was business. It was part of the price they had to pay. In the end, the money would be worth it.

Leonard turned off the evening news, picked up his pipe and reached in his shirt pocket for the tobacco pouch. It wasn't there. He gritted his teeth and shook his head. He had mislplaced it again. He picked up the morning paper off the throw pillow and saw the edge of the pouch between the cushions. He retrieved the small leather pouch containing the black Cavendish and carried it outside to the front porch.

It was a perfect evening. There was a slight breeze, the humidity was low, and the setting sun was cooling things off nicely. The locust were just beginning to drone, and the smell of a newly cut alfalfa field mixed with the aroma of some nearby wildflowers.

Leonard sat on the bench swing and began to fill his pipe. Linda would insist they go on a walk if she were with him. They would wait until the sun was about an inch above the horizon and go the long route. Sometimes they would drop in and visit friends along the way, but most of the time, they would just enjoy the evening and talk as they strolled down a country road. It's funny what he missed. For years and years every time she drafted him into taking a walk, he would try to think of some excuse to not go, and then reluctantly agree. Now that she was gone, he would give away all his possessions to be able to spend one evening walking with her.

Leonard lit his pipe, rested his head on the back of the bench, closed his eyes, and stretched his legs. He didn't hear the car stop in the drive.

"You look a little too relaxed," Leonard heard a soft voice coming from the bottom of his porch steps. He opened his eyes slowly. Could it be? Maybe he was imagining things. He leaned forward, took the pipe from his mouth, and grinned widely.

"Hello, Elaine," he said in reply. "If there's one thing I'm good at," he added, "it's knowing how to relax." He stood and motioned Elaine to come up the stairs. "Good to see you. Come on up and have a seat. Can I get you some tea? Lemonade?"

"Some lemonade would be nice," Elaine said nodding her head. She held out her hand to give Leonard a packet. "I was driving by Karo," she said, "and I thought I would just drop off the results of the Wilson pre-assessment." Leonard took the packet from her. "Thanks. I can get an early start on that tonight."

Elaine took a seat on the bench as Leonard hurried into the house. "Would tea be all right?" he called loudly from the kitchen. "I just remembered I don't have any lemonade mix." There was the sound of a cabinet door opening and closing quickly. "I found some instant tea," he shouted.

"Tea will be fine," Elaine answered. "Don't go to any trouble. I know what it's like to have unannounced visitors. I probably should have called. I hope you don't mind."

"No problem at all," Leonard said as he backed his way through the screen door with a glass in each hand and a half-filled pitcher under his arm. "I found a pitcher in the fridge," he announced proudly. He gave the cleaner of the two glasses to Elaine and placed the pitcher on the porch railing. He found himself standing in front of the bench. He hesitated. Should he sit next to her on the bench? Would that be too forward? But if he sat on the railing or the steps would he be sending her a message that he wasn't really pleased to see her? My God, he was thinking too much. Why did he do so much thinking when she was around? Why did he worry about every word he said?

Elaine took a hearty swig and looked up to see Leonard still standing. She scooted over on the bench to make room for him. Leonard sighed inwardly that the decision had been made for him, and took his place next to her.

"So I heard you took over the football team," she said with a tone of genuine curiosity.

"More like drafted into it," Leonard said. "Riley was in a real pinch, and it was either me or cancel the season. Promise me you'll come to a game," Leonard added spontaneously.

"I promise," Elaine smiled when she answered. She paused and took another drink. "I guess I didn't think someone like you would be interested in something like that," she said before her next drink.

Leonard raised his eyebrows and feigned offense. "Someone like me?" he said with a smile. "Why would you think someone like me would not be interested in coaching football?"

Elaine laughed slightly and shook her head as if to apologize. "I don't mean anything bad by it," she said. "It's just that you seem to be someone who would be more involved with books and ideas than sports."

"I'm a very balanced man," Leonard quipped. "Like the ancient Greeks, I strive to improve my body, mind and spirit every day." He suddenly worried if he hadn't come off as pompous. "Besides," he added quickly, "I am enjoying it."

"See what I mean?" Elaine held the tea in her lap. "How many people would invoke the ancient Greek culture and tie it to coaching football?" This time she giggled slightly.

Leonard laughed at himself as well. "That is kind of strange," he said as he took a sip of his tea. He stared at her and was suddenly struck to silence by how beautiful she was. For a moment all he could do was stare. He could not pull his gaze away from this stunning creature sitting right next to him.

What was happening? How could it happen? Could he let it happen? He had to look away, or he would say something he would regret later. He had to look away from her beautiful face or he would blurt out something stupid or he would try to kiss her. He dropped his eyes from hers and stared at his tea while he stirred the ice with his finger.

"It's just that…" Elaine hesitated as she spoke. "I don't see much about sports that impresses me. Well not sports, per se, but so many of the athletes act as if they are four years old. I would like to have a bumper sticker on my car with the symbols of all the sports on it, and a boldface type that says "I DON'T WORSHIP PETULANT CHILDREN."

Leonard took a long drink and nodded his head.

"Think about it for a minute," Elaine seemed glad to continue. "How does a four year old act? They are self-centered, impatient, demanding, and whine when they don't get their way. How many times have I seen the same behavior during a game on television? And it's not just the athletes. We're becoming a society of four-year olds. What is road rage but a four year old throwing a tantrum?"

"I agree there are many adults who don't act like adults," Leonard said. "But don't you think "worship" is a strong word?" Leonard asked.

Elaine took another sip and thought for a moment. "Think about it this way," she said and returned the cup to her lap. "We have television stations that devote themselves around the clock to celebrities and athletes. And the sad thing is, there are people who spend all the time they can at the foot of that alter. If that isn't worship, what is?"

"You make it sound," Leonard gathered his words, "like the great mass of people have such shallow, empty lives, that they feel they must get some of their own identity from someone famous, or some team, to make them feel better about themselves."

"Or maybe," Elaine responded, "our definition of "hero" has changed. We don't respect others like we used to. Our society doesn't respect its politicians, scientists, clergy, educators, or even the elderly. By default, the only groups left to model after are entertainers and athletes. How sad is that?"

Leonard nodded in agreement, and once again, he found himself staring at one of the most beautiful faces in the world. He was seeing a passion and a depth in her he had only dreamed would be there. A smile came over him. "So you don't see any value in sports?" he asked.

"Oh, no," Elaine reacted as though she had suddenly offended Leonard. "Oh, no." She brought her hand to her mouth. "I'm sorry," she said sounding truly contrite. "I think sports are good entertainment. It's fun, like a movie or a symphony. I might watch a game on television and those athletes will entertain me for a couple of hours. But when the game is over, they have absolutely no affect on my life, nor should they."

"It's funny you should mention the symphony," Leonard said." I have season tickets to the Wichita symphony orchestra, and I really enjoy the concerts. Do you attend regularly?"

Elaine sat up and grabbed Leonard's arm in one motion. 'Yes I do." She exclaimed. "Actually they are my parent's seats, but I get to use them four or five times during the year." She took her arm off of his. "Perhaps I'll see you at a concert some time."

Leonard didn't mind her hand on his arm. In fact, it felt good. Just the fact that a beautiful woman like Elaine would sit with him and feel comfortable enough to do that almost made him giddy. What was he thinking? How absurd. How could he be turned into a teenager by one touch?

"I hope we do," he said sincerely. "But let me use the symphony as an example of what we are talking about. Besides the beautiful music, one of the reasons I go there is to see and hear other people do things I can never do. I will never be able to play the cello like they do. I will never be able to sing Beethoven's ninth the way they do. I admire their ability. I suppose some of the reasons people love to see some tall man dunk a basketball is because it's something they will never be able to do."

"Yes," Elaine agreed, "but we are such a celebrity culture that many in our country don't leave it there. They want to wear the same clothes, buy the same stuff, and in general imitate the celebrity. That's where the worship factor comes in."

"Maybe," Leonard shook his head in agreement, "maybe what we need is not better athletes and celebrities, but better fans. Fans who love their game enough to stay away from the stadium, fans who would turn off the television and send a message that they are not sheep."

"You seem to agree so much with me," Elaine said in a confused tone, "and yet you are coaching a football team. Do you understand my confusion?"

Leonard sat his glass of tea on the porch railing, and nodded his head. "Why am I coaching?" He brought his hands together in front of him and rubbed his palms together. "Given that I agree that many celebrities and athletes in this world are, as you say, "petulant children" who are glorified by a society that only likes winners. Why would I choose to be a part of that? That's a good question."

Elaine began her own smile. She too was not disappointed in the depth of passion she saw before her. His disclaimer at the beginning of the conversation about improving body, mind and soul looked like it may be true. She was genuinely impressed by him. It only increased his attractiveness.

"I think the camaraderie is the main thing everyone in sports remembers," Leonard began. "There will be memories and friendships formed by the members of this team that will last the rest of their lives. Then there's the self-discipline and persistence which will be life long lessons." He paused for a moment, as if gathering his thoughts. "But I guess what it al boils down to with me is how beautiful it is when people work together. A team at top form is a wonder to behold. Shoulder to shoulder working toward a common goal, sharing the burdens and the joys, picking each other up when they fall, appreciating each other, and knowing in the long run that pride comes from the effort and not from the result."

Leonard paused again and looked at Elaine as if he had known her all his life. "I guess when I see that, I get the feeling that maybe this is the closest we come to knowing what God meant us to be like."

They were both silent for a moment as their eyes held each other. Leonard stared at that beautiful face and this time he spoke before thinking. "How could someone like you not be married?" he asked. He instantly apologized and shook his head in regret.

Elaine was taken aback for a moment, but she was not upset.

"It's okay," she said calmly. "I've had my opportunities, but I guess I'm not willing to settle. It's not been easy. But I have yet to find the right one. It's been hard. I know life can be easy; all you have to do is lower your standards."

Their eyes locked again. Neither spoke. Elaine knew her intuitions had been right. Here was a man of depth and strength. She would love to spend more time with him. She would love to get to know him better. She would love to kiss him. She leaned in toward him hoping he would do likewise. She reached her hand softly under his chin and pulled his face toward hers.

Leonard pulled back. His mind was whirling. He had to break away. He turned his head around and looked at the sunset. His life was comfortable. His routines were comfortable. He had resigned the rest of his life to them. He didn't need anything to upset them. He wasn't ready. He had accepted the fact that love would never find him again. He had just crawled out of the bottom of the Grand Canyon for Christ's sake. Why would he risk falling back down to the bottom?

Neither spoke for a long moment. The locust began to fill the evening with their modulating, continual chords.

"Elaine," Leonard did not turn to face her. "I'm sorry. I'm not sure. You are a wonderful woman," he said in a distant voice. "I think you are very nice, but I don't think I should lead you to believe there can be anything between us. I just don't know." He finally turned to look at her. "Maybe I'm not ready."

Elaine said nothing. She looked down. "I…I didn't mean we should have a relationship," she tried to hide it, but her face showed disappointment and embarrassment. "I just thought," she stammered, "maybe we could get to know each other. I'm sorry if I misled you into thinking I was looking for something more." She bit her lower lip and wondered to herself if, like Hamlet's mother, she had just protested too much.

They both sat silently on the bench for a moment. The sound of the locust grew louder. Leonard was looking for a way to tell her how afraid he was, and Elaine was trying to convince herself that she did not feel what she felt.

Leonard looked at her again. She was more beautiful than ever. He so desperately wanted to pull her close, push her hair back from over her eyes, lean down and kiss her. What was stopping him? His heart was heavy and his head was spinning. Had he done the right thing? Did he think that an opportunity with a woman like this came everyday? What code was he living by? How many times had he imagined an opportunity like this to be alone with her, get to know her, and tell her how he felt? Was he being noble, or was he being a coward?

"Well," Elaine said as she rose from the bench. "Thanks for the tea, but I'd better get going." She handed him the glass.

"Drop by again," Leonard said out of habit as he took the glass. He knew she wouldn't. He wanted to ask her to stay, but he couldn't. She began walking down the stairs to the sidewalk. He wanted to shout to her to stop, but he didn't. He watched as she quietly got into her car, started it, and drove away.

Leonard stood statue-like, holding two empty glasses of tea. "I think I love you," he finally said aloud. "But I don't know what to do about it." Only the locust answered him.

Greg came in the front door exhausted. Football practice had been long and difficult. He walked into the kitchen and went directly to the refrigerator. He pulled the milk carton from the top shelf, opened it and began to drink. Coach Davis seemed to be in a bad mood today, and that was unusual because coach Davis was hardly ever in a bad mood.

Greg felt good about the season. He was probably going to start as a tackle on both sides of the ball. He believed most of the team was working hard, and more importantly, this year they seemed to care about what happened during the season.

He drank almost all the contents in the half-gallon container before he remembered he was supposed to use a glass. He brought it down from his mouth and looked around. He didn't see or hear anyone. Dad must still be at work, and his mother must be out in the garden. He took a final drink, put the milk back in the refrigerator, and walked over to the kitchen table to check the mail. He glanced out the kitchen window above the sink.

He saw his mother in her familiar gardening clothes: faded jeans, thin cotton gloves, red checkered shirt and an old yellow wide-brimmed straw hat. She found peace in the fall garden. For a moment, Greg just watched her. He saw her lips moving and knew she was singing to herself. Moments like this are what she still fought for. It was a beautiful autumn day, the breeze and sun warmed and cooled her at the same time. Her hands were in the dirt and her voice was singing to nobody.

A quick burst of wind suddenly blew her hat off. Only the string tied under her chin kept if from flipping down the row of flowers. A bald head underneath suddenly revealed itself. Patches of dark were evident where her hair was trying to grow back.

His mom postponed her weeding for a second and pulled the hat back on. Chemotherapy be damned. The gardening must be done.

Greg dropped the mail to the counter. His mother was going to die. The doctors couldn't save her. His father the preacher couldn't save her. There would be no miracle cure. She would slowly waste away. How could such a thing happen to a good Christian family? God was not good. God was weak. God was a coward.

Greg wiped a tear from his cheek and headed toward the back porch door. He thought he would go pull weeds for a while.

“What does question 27 mean, coach?” Alan raised his hand. Although almost everybody on the team was finished, Alan was still working on his rules test.

Leonard put his glasses on, flipped his copy to the third page and ran his finger down to number 27. He read aloud, “must the receiver signal a fair catch to eligible for a free kick?”

“What’s that?” Alan asked.

Leonard slid his glasses down his nose and looked over them at his charge. “Did you read that section of the rule book like you were supposed to?” He would bet that Alan had read it but did not understand.

“Yeah,” Alan shrugged his shoulders,” but I don’t remember nothing about it.”

Leonard was tempted to correct the double negative, but one thing at a time was always better with Alan. He walked over to Alan’s desk and took a seat next to him. “Any time during the game if there is a kick, say like a punt or a kick-off, three things can happen. First, it can be returned by the receiving team, second if there is a fair catch, the receiving team begins with the ball at that point, or third the receiving team can choose to “free kick” the ball. In order to do that they give up the right to try for a first and ten, and the ball is placed on the kicking tee at that spot. It’s just like a kick-off, and if the kicker gets it through the uprights, his team gets three points.”

"Is that a new rule, coach?" Alan asked.

Leonard smiled slightly. "No, Alan," he said. "It's a very old rule. It's just that nobody ever uses it anymore. I don't think I've heard of a team choosing to free kick in thirty years."

Alan marked the answer and handed over his test. "Done, coach," he said. "Thanks for the help."

Leonard walked back to the front desk. Almost everybody had paired off for their chess matches. He had organized a tournament for them, and had been pleasantly surprised how well the team had responded. In fact, if he ever suggested they skip a day he would hear complaints. The only protests now were about the silence. The team wanted to listen to music while they played. There had been dozens of suggestions, but no agreement on what they should listen to. Leonard knew there would never be unanimous consent, so he took the matter into his own hands.

"I've solved the music problem," he announced as he put Alan's test on the desk. "Since we have absolutely no agreement from you guys as to what kind of music we should listen to, I have decided to act like Solomon, and throw out all of your choices."

There were a few gasps and even some audible moans. They knew what kind of music coach Davis listened to. They knew what was coming next.

"I have chosen for today," Leonard held up a compact disk for all to see, "Brandenburg concertos 1, 2, and 3. Tomorrow we will get numbers 4, 5, and 6. The team's reaction was predictable, and it did not match Leonard's enthusiasm.

"Come on, coach," someone called. "That stuff will put us to sleep."

"It will help you concentrate," Leonard countered.

"I don't want to listen to any elevator music," came another call.

"There isn't an elevator in the country that plays Bach," Leonard said.

Leonard ignored the wailing and gnashing of teeth, and took the disk out. "Why do you listen to that stuff, Coach?" The question hung in the air. "A hundred years from now," Leonard said without pause, "while people are reading in their history books about music of this period," he turned and waved the disk, "they will be listening to this."

"This sucks," came a whisper from the back of the room.

Leonard turned and put the disk in the player. "Here's what I want you to do," he said. "I want you to ignore the music. Pretend it's not there. Go ahead and get started on your chess game, and don't let the music bother you." The first few bars began flowing through the air like a mountain stream. Leonard turned the volume down. "Just go ahead with your matches," he said as he waved his hand for them to begin. "Pretend the music isn't there."

"Elevator music," Leonard heard again when he turned toward the desk.

There were a few more grumbles, but most of them had already begun jousting on their checkered fields. Within minutes, the only sounds were the occasional exasperated cry of someone being taught the foolishness of his decision, and the lilt of sixteenth notes floating over everyone's head.

School had been going for two weeks now, and the first game was in two days. The time had gone so fast. Leonard didn't know if the team was ready to play its first game or not, but he had enjoyed the coaching so far.

"Coach Davis?" Leonard looked up to see Riley outside the door of the classroom. With him was a young man smaller than Riley. He had blond hair, a sharp chin, a sharper nose and deep set blue eyes. Leonard had never seen him before. Leonard rose from the desk and met them in the hall.

"Coach Davis," Riley said pointing to the young man. "This is a foreign exchange student from Albania. His name is"… Riley paused and looked at the Transylvanian gnome, "let me get this right. His name is Ilir. Ilir Kucoj, and he wants to play football."

Leonard smiled and extended his hand. It was eagerly accepted. Leonard wondered if he were to inherit a player, why he couldn't be large and strong. Instead, he saw a skinny, half-pint who wouldn't know a football from a frozen turkey. "Welcome to Karo," Leonard said. The kid had a disarming smile, and Leonard soon found his own fake grin quickly becoming real.

"So, Ilir, have you ever played American football before?" Leonard instantly thought he had just asked the most preposterous question of the last forty years of his life.

"No," Ilir said using his hands as he talked. "In Albania we do not play the American football. We play soccer. But I wish to play with the American football. It is to me interesting."

"It is to me too," Leonard said with as sigh and a smile.

"Why don't you go on into the "football practice"," Riley said to Ilir with a grin.

Leonard chose to ignore the quip. "Besides," Riley continued, "I have something to discuss with Mr. Davis."

Brad Hoeffen walked up to the door when Coach Davis waved him over. Ilir was taken aback. "You play chess with the American football?" Ilir was astonished as he stepped into the room. "Sure," Brad said surveying the room himself. "Haven't you ever heard of Bobby Fisher? He was a linebacker."

Leonard quickly closed the door. He'd heard enough.

Riley turned slowly toward the window. "Edgar Fortus made a motion last night that the board close the school and consider consolidation. The board voted 4 to 3 to take the matter under consideration while they look at other schools we could consolidate with." Riley continued staring out the window. "By Thanksgiving," he said in a distant voice, "they will probably vote to close the school."

Leonard looked out the window as well. For several minutes they both stood staring. Neither spoke. Finally, and without a word, Riley slowly turned and made his way back to the office. Leonard spent a few more minutes at the window before he went back into football practice.

Leonard led the team out of the locker room for practice. He stopped for a second, took a deep breath and closed his eyes. The hot days of August were coming to an end and the promise of a cool fall hung in the air. Leonard loved the fall. He loved the weather, the changing of the leaves, the new school year and the start of another football season. At that moment he couldn't imagine himself doing anything else.

He opened his eyes and turned when he heard a pick-up pull around the corner and head toward him. William Roundtree was approaching. Leonard waved. In the back of the truck, Leonard could see about a dozen large drum barrels, each one painted a bright red. The truck slowed to a stop, the dust settled quickly, and William swatted a fly out of the cab.

"The landfill is way out on K-12!" Leonard said as he approached.

William stepped out of the cab and motioned toward the barrels. "I brought you some new players," he said. "Some of them are probably better than the ones you are going to start tomorrow night."

"If they can block and tackle," Leonard answered, "I'll take them." He looked at the barrels, paused and turned to William. "What do you have in mind?"

William reached into the back and pulled one out. "George Platnik over in Stone township said I could have them until the season is over, so I got eleven of them. They won't move, but you can use them to show alignments and formations." He lifted another from his truck. "I figured they were better than imagining someone was there."

"I'm impressed," Leonard said and called the team over to the truck. "Take these out to the field and set them up on the twenty yard line in a 5-2 defense with a strong safety on the tight end side," he instructed. The team quickly emptied the contents of the truck bed and carried the barrels out to the field.

"Good idea, William," Leonard said appreciatively.

"It might get better," William offered. "If we fill the bottom half of each barrel with sand or dirt, they might be able to block them. It would give them a better feel for the blocking patterns. They'd get a better sense of how things will be in the game if they get to push something around. Imagination and brains are one thing, but the guys on Friday night wearing different colors are going to be real. Simpson High has a good team."

Leonard noticed that William said "we."

"I wish we could open the season with an easier opponent," Leonard said. "These guys have been kicked in the teeth for so many years it would be nice to play a weak team as our first opponent."

"Looks to me like tomorrow night will be a chance to see how far we've come," William said as he leaned against the truck. Leonard noticed again the third person plural inclusive pronoun. "There's a buzz around town," William continued. "People are talking about chess, track, study hall, flat tires and Bach. Most of them think it's pretty weird damn stuff."

Leonard suppressed a smile.

"Most people don't understand it," William finished, "but they figure they'll give you a chance."

"That's very gracious of them," Leonard said through a grin.

"Well you and I both know that the average guy knows as much about football as he knows about politics. He knows you're supposed to win. But have him describe the difference between a veer option, a wishbone option, a trap option and a speed option and they couldn't tell you to save their ass."

Leonard nodded. "I know I've had the team do a lot of different things," he said. "But I'm doing what I think is right, and I'm doing it the only way I know how."

"I know you are," William said. "I'm not one of the critics. And even though you have been doing some damn strange stuff, I'll tell you what I see. I see improvement. I see purpose. I think," he said pointing out toward the practice field, "I think they are starting to believe in what you're doing. Next you've got to get them to believe in themselves." William paused. "That may be the hardest part."

"What if it all crashes to the ground tomorrow?," Leonard asked. "What if we are humiliated once again? Will we go back to our old ways?"

William could tell that his friend was genuinely concerned. "I believe," he said as he put his hand on Leonard's shoulder," you are going to break the streak this year. It may not be tomorrow, but it will happen. One Friday this season, there will be a celebration in Karo that will have people dancing in the streets." William folded his arms on his chest and nodded out toward the practice field. "That's a good group of young men you have out there, and they will follow your lead. All you have to do is take them in the right direction."

"Coach." Alan called from amid the barrels. "If they line up in a 5-2, are the linebackers going to play over the inside shoulder of the guards, or will they be head up?"

Leonard took his hat off, rubbed his forehead, and looked at William. "What do you think?" he asked. "Does Simpson run their 52 with the linebackers in or out?"

"Depends on the strong safety," William answered without hesitation. "If the strong safety is on his side, that linebacker will more than likely play inside shoulder. But if the strong safety is on the opposite side of the linebacker, he will probably shade to the outside."

Leonard nodded in agreement and put his hat back on. "So if they flip the strong safety toward the formation, we can expect their linebackers to adjust accordingly."

"I believe so," William said.

Leonard nodded again and looked out toward the field. "Be there in a minute," he shouted to Alan. He suddenly turned toward William. "You have a good knowledge of the game," he said, "and there isn't a player on the team who doesn't know and respect you." Leonard added.

"Before you ask," William interrupted, "the answer is yes. I would like to help you coach the team." William grinned from ear to ear. "I've been wanting to ask you for several days if I could."

"That's great," Leonard exclaimed. "I could sure use the help.

William's smile continued. In fact, it turned into a chuckle. "You know," he said through his laughter, "the last time I made a damn fool decision like this, I ended up sleeping in the jungle,"

"You'll survive this too," Leonard said.

There was a long pause as they both stared out toward the field. "I can't explain it," William said slowly, "but something tells me that this season is going to be special, and I want to be part of it." He looked at his friend and stuck out his hand. "You've got yourself a coach," he said. "Let's go get practice started."

"The fun's just starting," Leonard said.

Two dozen fans were scattered around the bleachers as the band played the national anthem. The watermelon feed that was supposed to bring in the crowd for the first game had not been a success. A livestock tank half full of ice water and watermelons sat unattended in the parking lot. A half dozen cheerleaders did their routines to a mute, apathetic crowd. When the team took the field, there was a spattering of applause.

The game began with an onside kick. Simpson High fooled everyone and recovered the ball on the Karo 39 yard line. Two plays later there was a mix-up in the secondary and a Simpson receiver stood alone in the end-zone as the ball sailed to him for an easy touchdown. They added a two point conversion. On the ensuing kickoff, the ball bounced off the chest of the Karo receiver and Simpson High recovered. This time, in one play, a sweep carried them into the end zone. The two point conversion was good and within a span of 54 seconds, Simpson led the game 16-0.

The second quarter saw a long snap sail over the head of the Karo punter, another fumble, and interception against the Eagles. Each led to another score. When they retired for half-time, the Karo Eagles trailed 35-0.

Leonard thought his team was playing hard, but they were making so many mistakes. Their adjustments at half-time helped some, but two more turnovers, and a stumbling secondary kept the scoreboard busy for Simpson. By the time the carnage was over, the difference on the scoreboard was 56-0. By any measure, the game had been a disaster.

Leonard followed the team slowly past the stands to the locker room. A fan standing on the last row of the bleachers cupped his hands and yelled at Leonard as he walked by. "Where the hell did you learn to coach?"

Leonard suddenly wondered if the fan was right. Maybe he wasn't cut out for this job. Why was he wasting his time pretending to be a football coach. Maybe the adage was right that there is no fool like an old fool. He followed the team into the locker room and walked to the front as they sat quietly on the basketball bleachers.

Leonard wondered what he could say to make things better. Had he misled them? Had he set them up for failure? Had he expected too much from them? "No," he thought to himself, "but one shouldn't expect a starving man to suddenly eat steak."

"Let me have everyone's attention," he said quietly. About half the eyes slowly rose to meet his. "The last few weeks we have talked about winning that first game and ending the streak," he paused. "But that was wrong. We're not ready to win that first game yet. We must crawl before we walk, and walk before we run."

Leonard took off his hat and paced a little. "Fifty years ago there was a cargo ship carrying fifty tons of iron ore across Lake Superior on its way to Michigan, when it was hit by a sudden and fierce November storm. The ship tried to make it back to port but couldn't. It was such a terrible storm that the cold wind and the thirty foot waves finally broke the ship in two. It sank to the bottom about two miles off shore."

This time when he looked out at the team, almost every eye was on him. "There were twenty-nine sailors on that ship," Leonard continued. "And when it went down there were three different groups trying to stay alive in icy, rolling water. The first group began to blame the captain for their situation. "He did this wrong," and "he did that wrong," they said. Soon they were all pointing fingers at each other and arguing over whose fault it was. Eventually, exhausted, they sank below the surface.

Now every eye was on him. "The second group," he continued, "immediately began to feel sorry for themselves. They raised their eyes to heaven and called, "Why me? Why did this ship have to sink? I'm a good man, I haven't done anything to deserve this!" They moaned and groaned and complained that such a terrible thing could happen to them. They were still complaining as they sank, exhausted, to the bottom of the lake."

"But there was a third group," Leonard spoke louder now. "It was the smallest of the three, but they immediately began to swim toward shore. They knew that every minute they wasted on blame would be one less minute they could use to get to safety. Neither did they waste any time feeling sorry for themselves. What had happened to them was terrible, but there was nothing they could do about it. They knew that every minute they wasted in self-pity was one less minute they could use to get to safety."

"Not everyone in that third group made it to shore, but some of them did, and when they were found, the rescue workers were amazed that anybody survived. It was so hard to believe that anybody could do what they had done, and the rescuers asked that very question. "How could you swim such a distance in the middle of a raging winter storm"? they asked. "I didn't," came the answer. "I just swam the next wave."

Leonard looked over the faces staring back at him. "Somewhere in the last five years," he said, "this ship sank. And some of us have been treading water ever since. Today we start heading for the shore. We're not going to worry about how far we've come or how far we still have to go. We only know that if we continue to swim the next wave, we will eventually find ourselves standing on the shore."

Leonard waited for questions or comments. There were none. "Go hit the showers," he said quietly and the team shuffled off toward the locker room.

"Report all injuries to me," William added as he walked up to Leonard.

"That was quite a story," William said to Leonard when the last player disappeared behind the locker room doors. "Is it true?"

"Yes it is," Leonard said as he began walking toward the locker room. "Except in the real event, they all drowned."

William pulled the bus over the hill and slowed for the next stop. "Shit!" he said under his breath. As usual, Nicholas and Russell were there, and as usual, they were teasing those damned dogs. He would have to talk to them again and let them know how angry he was.

Hazel Everett bought the three Rotweillers two years ago to protect her property, even though, as far as William could tell, she didn't have anything worth stealing. She had just divorced her husband for cheating on her one too many times, and she didn't like the idea of living out in the country alone. She secretly hoped her ex would come back one day so she could sic the three musketeers on him. That's what she called them, so they were appropriately named Porthos, Aramis, and D'Artagnan.

Nicholas and Russell dropped their rocks when they heard the bus coming over the hill, gathered their books, and ran over to their drive. The bus stopped, the dust settled, and they bounded up the steps.

"What did I tell you?" William nearly shouted when they made it to the top step. "Didn't I tell you not to bother those dogs again? Didn't I tell you to leave them alone?"

Nicholas opened his mouth as if he wanted to argue, thought better of it, and lowered his head. "Yes, Mr. Roundtree."

"He threw rocks at 'em," Russell chimed in from behind.

"Shut up, Russell." Nicholas elbowed his little brother in the side of the head.

"That's enough," William commanded and reached out a massive hand between the two. The altercation was over before it began. "Now get back to your seats," he ordered.

Russell scooted past Nicholas after delivering a quick elbow to the side of his brother and headed for the back of the bus. Nicholas started to follow but was pulled back by his coat and found himself face to face with a very unhappy bus driver.

"Look at me son," William said with genuine concern. "One of those dogs is as big as you, and there are three of them. Do you know what could happen to you?" William paused and shook his head slowly. "You have to quit teasing them. You have to leave them alone. It could be dangerous. I mean it. I don't ever want to come over this hill and see you bothering them again. Do you hear me? Do you understand?"

There was a quick nod yes.

"I mean it," William repeated as he let go of the coat. "I mean it," he said again. "Never again."

"Yes, sir," Nicholas answered and lowered his eyes again.

"Now go get in your seat," William ordered as he patted Nicholas on the rear and sent him down the aisle. He looked at his watch. 7:35. Damn! He was behind schedule. He still had to stop at the Foster house, the Blake house, and the Ronnenfeld's before the route was over. He ground the gearbox until he found granny gear and began to roll down the gravel road. He was going to have to replace the clutch in this thing as soon as he could find the time.

“Don’t leave your books in the living room!” the shout came from the kitchen. “You’re eighteen years old. You know we don’t use that room unless we have company, important company. That whole room is an off white, a cream, and it is too hard to clean. We’re probably going to replace it sometime this winter, but that doesn’t mean you can use it as a closet. Josh! Do you hear me? Joshua!”

“I heard you mom,” Josh called from the sacred room. He knew when his mom used his full first name she was becoming agitated. He had put his book bag on the plastic sheet that covered the couch before heading off to the bathroom. He should have dropped it to the floor instead.

He picked up the backpack to carry it with him just as his mom came around the corner. She was carrying a wooden spoon.

“I’ve got spaghetti on the stove and now I have to interrupt my cooking. You’ve got to use more common sense. Why don’t you have common sense like your brother? What’s that smell? Turn around and let me smell your jacket. Come back here. Is that cigarettes? Do I smell cigarettes? I will not allow smokers in this house. Smokers are weak, ignorant people. Do you hear me? Tell me you haven’t been smoking. You haven’t been smoking have you?”

“I haven’t been smoking,” Josh said as he turned back around. “Some of the guys I hang with smoke.”

“Well, I don’t like it,” his mother fumed. “You shouldn’t be around them. I'm disappointed in your choice of friends. Some of those guys you know are not very high class. Did you ever take a look at their lawns? My God! Nothing but weeds and patches of dirt. They have no class. How can you stand to be around them?"

"They're my friends," Josh protested.

"Well, I'm disappointed in them, and I'm disappointed in you. You should show more character than to be with a group of thugs who smoke cigarettes and don't have any class. You should see some of the cars they drive!"

"Just forget it," Josh began to walk away.

"Don't walk away from me young man. I have raised you to be better than this. I'm disappointed in you. Your father and I have worked hard so you can have a good life and we don't want to sit around and see you throw it all away. Why can't you be more like your brother? He never hung around with people who had no class. He always had good report cards. He wouldn't be seen with a smoker."

"I'm going to my room," Josh said and started up the stairs.

"No you're not young man," his mother called after him. "You come back down here and listen to your mother." Josh continued up the stars, but stopped about half way up. "I don't know what has gotten into you this year," his mom continued. "Your grades are down, I can't believe some of the girls you are dating, and now you're hanging around with the low class of the town. It's like you don't want to do anything right. How are you going to get into a good college? We'll be lucky if you even get into college. Your brother will have a law degree and you will be repairing refrigerators. How are you going to be a success? You won't. You'll be at the corner bar wasting your life away."

"Just let me go to my room," Josh said through clenched teeth.

"Your clothes smell like smoke," she pointed up the stairs with the wooden spoon. "Go change your clothes so I can wash them. You just wait until your father gets home. If you think I have a problem with your attitude, just wait till you talk to him. You are nothing like your brother. Why do you disappoint us so much?"

Josh finally turned and made it to his room. He closed the door and sat by the window. He could use a drink. Tonight he would get with Wanda and have her older brother buy them some beer. Maybe he could score some weed. Then he could party all night. He opened the window and looked out at the treetops.

"Maybe I'll take up smoking," he said with a laugh.

“You had better turn those things,” Leonard motioned toward the grill, “or they won’t be edible.”

William walked over to take a look at the three sirloins. “You just don’t understand the Indian way,” he said. “Who knows more about cooking outside over an open flame? This skill has been handed down from generation to generation. Hundreds of years ago, my forefathers probably fed your forefathers some buffalo steaks on the barbie.” William made sure Leonard wasn’t looking and turned them anyway.

“You’re using propane gas for God’s sake,” Leonard said flatly and took another sip of his iced tea. It was Sunday evening at the Roundtree house. Leonard wondered if either William or Samantha knew how important these Sunday evenings were to him. In the winter it would be stew or something hot. The warmer weather would usually find them out in the back yard enjoying the sunset.

“Leonard put his tea on the ground next to his folding chair. “I’m just not sure now if I did the right thing,” he said. “After what happened last Friday, I don’t know if I can coach this team or not. We fell apart out there, and I think it may be my fault.”

William turned from the grill and returned to his chair. He took a long drink form his tea but said nothing. Leonard began to fill his pipe. There was a long silence interrupted by the occasional crackle of open flame on the steaks.

"Have you ever tried to lose weight?" William asked.

Leonard lit his pipe, blew out the match, and turned toward his friend. "Why?" he asked. "What's that got to do with anything?"

"I knew a guy when I was at Wichita State who lost 40 pounds in one year," William said as he leaned back in his chair. "Kept it off too."

Leonard picked up his tea from the grass and took another drink.

"He never had a diet, didn't count calories, and had no idea how many points this or that food was worth. He checked his weight once a year on New Year's Day," William continued. "Then after that, he didn't even bother to check it anymore because it wasn't important."

Leonard took a long draw on his pipe. "Let me get this straight," he said between puffs. "He only weighed himself once a year, and then he decided he didn't have to do that anymore. How did he know he had lost weight?"

"With a stopwatch," William said. He got up to check the steaks. They needed to be turned again. "His goal was to run a six-minute mile. He knew that anybody out of shape could never do that, so he was determined to do it. When he could run a mile in six minutes, he would be in shape. It took him three years to do it, but he finally was able to break that six minute barrier. He still runs about that time today." William turned the last steak and went back to his chair. "He tells me his time almost every time I see him."

Leonard took another long draw. He understood. Maybe most people achieved their important goals accidentally. Sometimes it didn't make sense, and maybe it seemed too simple, but it was true. If he put winning as his goal, he would obsess and fret for the next two months, get the team wound up as tight as a drum, and probably lose every game. But if he kept busy simply trying to improve them a little bit at a time, he would keep them loose, and the wins would come as a result. What was his goal? To win games, or make better young men.

"I know what I want out of this year," William said. "I want to help these young men pull themselves up off the floor. They have been down so long and kicked around so much, they have forgotten what it is like to stand on their own two feet. They have forgotten what is like to face the world with their heads up. There are too many like them in the world, cowering and complacent, not willing or able to pay the price required to be a man."

William took a short drink and continued. "I want to be there when they face the world again on even terms. I want to be there when they are no longer ashamed of who they are, or where they are from. That's what I want," William said nodding his head. "I want to be there when they learn how to stand tall."

"To face the world standing," Leonard said quietly. "What a noble goal," he said through another puff.

The screen door closed and the two of them looked at the back porch steps. Samantha was bringing out a vegetable tray.

"You have a call," she said to William as she approached.

William groaned. "Who is it?"

"I don't know," Samantha answered. "You'll have to find out for yourself."

"I'll tend the grill," Leonard said and headed toward the sizzling steaks. William walked slowly into the house.

Samantha cleared a corner of the table and set down the tray. Her skin was lighter than William's, but she had deeper brown eyes. Her amber skin complimented a full head of hair that could only be described as midnight black. She had a round face, round shoulders, and full round breasts. She always found the energy for the things she needed to do, and was overflowing with energy for the things she wanted to do.

"Now," she said without hesitation. "Tell me about this Elaine Simmons. I hear she came by to see you last week."

Leonard smiled inwardly. How could he expect a visitor to his front porch not to be noticed by at least one neighbor? "Small towns," he said in an exasperated voice. "She wasn't at my house more that twenty minutes and it's already around town." He sighed.

"Well," Samantha was not about to let it drop. "What do you think? Is there a chance of something starting?"

Leonard turned the steaks again. "I don't know," he said truthfully. "I don't think I could get back in the dating world. It's all too complicated for an old dog like me. Besides, I had my chance."

"It's been three years," Samantha said after a short pause. "Don't you think you have had enough time?"

"I don't know," Leonard spoke the truth again. "Maybe time doesn't make any difference. Maybe it does." Leonard checked the steaks once more. "Maybe it's best just to accept things as they are." Leonard's voice trailed off into silence.

Samantha spoke softly but sternly. "Linda was my friend, and I loved her too," she said. "We all miss her, and I know you will never be able to replace her. But you seem unwilling to pursue any further attempts at happiness. You seem unwilling to even try."

Leonard turned the steaks again. He didn't answer until they were all turned. "It's been three years," he began, "but there are still mornings when I hear her walking down the hall bringing me my morning cup of coffee. She would always bring me a cup of coffee when I was waking up. Her quiet time was in the morning and when that was over, rain or shine, winter or summer, she would bring me that cup of coffee. What a simple, unselfish act of love." Leonard stared at the grill. "I don't know if I could do dating today," he continued. "Today everything is quid pro quo. An unselfish act is seen as weakness."

Samantha took the fork from Leonard's hand, walked over to the grill, inspected the steaks, and began to take them off the grill. "These are done," she said and began to pile them on the plate.

"That's it?" he said. "These are done? No words of wisdom?" he queried.

"You have already decided," Samantha said as she filled the plate. "You have decided not to try again. You have the right to choose the difficult path. It is a very hard journey and a very lonely one. I wish you luck."

Samantha put the last steak on the plate and closed the lid of the grill. "You know it's kind of ironic," she said. "William has been trying so hard for years to let go of his past, and your are trying just as hard to hold on to yours." Samantha looked directly at Leonard. "I don't know if either one of you will succeed, but I do know this, when you are walking the floor at night because you can't sleep, you won't have anybody to blame but yourself."

Leonard didn't respond. He didn't know what to say. There was the familiar bang of the screen door, and they both saw William coming down the walk. "Goddamn telemarketers," he muttered as he approached.

Ilir held up his shoulder pads and looked at them with a questioning gaze. He glanced around to see how everyone else was putting the pads on and followed their lead. He put them on backwards. The drawstrings and clips to hold them on were nowhere to be found. They dangled behind him. He bent over, finally shook the pads off his shoulders and then put them on correctly. He copied the others as he tied the drawstrings and snapped the clips into place.

After years of practice, everybody else was able to pull their practice jersey over their pads with minimum effort. Not so with Ilir. His jersey stuck halfway down and would go no further. He struggled to pull it off and could not. He was caught with the jersey covering his head. Neither the jersey nor the shoulder pads would budge. Ilir began to thrash around with his arms trapped at his side. The empty sleeves flailed as he tried to free his arms. He looked like a headless scarecrow having an epileptic fit.

"Slow down there, turbo," Ilir heard a voice outside his cocoon. It was Greg. "You're going to give yourself a headache." Greg and Brad took hold of the jersey on each side, and with a grunt from Ilir, pulled it down. A small blond head appeared, smiling widely and swaying slightly from side to side.

"This American football has many unusual rules," he said still grinning. "I think I hope to learn them. I want to learn many things about the American life."

"Well, you've come to the right place." Greg nodded to Brad as he spoke. "Ain't that right, Brad?

"Hell, yes," Brad agreed. "But if you really want to learn about America, you have to know our culture, our traditions, and our songs."

"Especially our songs," Greg added enthusiastically. "The national anthem, the school song, and especially the team song."

"Oh, yeah," Brad took over. "To have an understanding of the American football, you need to know the official Karo football team song."

For a moment Ilir was lost in studied concentration. Then quickly a cautious smile flashed across his face. He smelled something fishy. "A football team has a song?" he asked. "Give me the break."

"No, it's true," Brad said seriously. "This tradition has been handed down from generation to generation in Karo. If you really want to be a part of the team, you will learn this song."

There was a slight pause. "What is this song?" Ilir posed the obvious question.

"Shall we teach him?" Greg looked at Brad. "Do you think he can learn it?"

Brad nodded approval and turned to Ilir. "I don't know if he can do it, but let's give it a try." Brad furrowed his brow, tilted his head up slightly, and spoke with complete sincerity. "Alright, Ilir. Let's see if you can learn these words." Brad raised his index finger and chanted in a syncopated, sing-song voice. "Come-ah, come-ah, down, dooby doo, down, down."

Greg nodded his approval. "Chilling," he said.

"What is it that you say?" Ilir asked seriously. "I do not have heard these words before."

Brad pointed his finger at Ilir. "If you want to be part of the team, you have to know the official team song. Now do you want to be part of the team or not?"

Ilir nodded enthusiastically that he did.

"Repeat after me," Brad raised his index finger again. "Come-ah, come-ah," he paused.

"Coma, coma," Ilir parroted.

"Down, dooby doo."

"Don, do, be, doe."

"Down, down."

"Don, don."

"Good job," Greg slapped Ilir on the shoulder. "You sound like a real American," Ilir grinned from ear to ear.

"You have to be able to sing it though," Brad said. "There's like a hundred verses, and you have to do that for all of them. Try again." Brad started again. "Come-ah, come-ah" and waited for Ilir to continue.

"Do dowby do," Ilir said. Brad shook his head no. Ilir tried again.

"Dow, don, don, doby," Brad shook his head again even more emphatically.

"Do, doby, don, don," Brad waved his hand in front of Ilir's face to make him stop.

"Down, dooby, do, down, down," Greg corrected.

"This song is important?" Ilir asked.

"Next to happy birthday," Brad answered, "It's the most popular song in the states." Greg nodded his concurrence. "Let's give him a little of what it should be," Greg said and counted to three. Immediately he was doing his best Neal Sedaka rendition as Brad sang he back-up with precision. "Don't take your love…away from me…don't you leave my heart in misery…after all that we've been through…breaking up is hard to do."

Brad motioned for Ilir to join him. "Come-ah, come-ah," He continued to sing background.

Ilir tried to quickly repeat what he heard. "Dow, doob, down…come dow…cow doo doo…"

The cow doo doo was too much and Greg and Brad burst out laughing. Brad laughed so hard he had to sit on the floor to keep from falling. Ilir was confused for a moment, and then he was laughing as well. Within seconds others gathered around. Soon the entire locker room was full of laughter. Most didn't know why, but they found themselves laughing all the same.

It was five minutes before the team was able to gather itself and head out to practice. Brad and Greg were determined that Ilir would lean all the words to the song, and Ilir thought he was well on his way to learning about America.

Leonard cleared the table and pulled chairs around it. There were five members on the Student Improvement Team, plus the referring teacher, so he would have to have at least six places. He decided to put seven chairs out in case a pair of teachers came in together and both wanted to discuss the same student. He put his notebook in the middle of the table.

His mind was racing. He would see Elaine again. He needed to talk to her. He needed to explain some things. He hoped she would be able to stay after the meeting. Maybe they could go out for a cup of coffee. Would that be considered a date? He hadn't been on a date in three years. Dating was a foreign word to him. He wasn't sure what the definition was. He wasn't sure about anything when it came to starting over. He was only sure bout one thing, he would like to talk to her again. Maybe they could get to know each other better. Maybe there was a chance that things could develop.

"Do you want some?" Leonard looked up to see Riley holding two cups. "Fresh from this morning," he said.

"No, thanks," Leonard said as he put the last chair in place. "I prefer coffee that is less than six hours old," he said.

Riley shrugged and walked over placing both cups on the table. "Maybe someone else will," he said as he took his seat. "Who's on the schedule for today?" he asked.

Leonard opened his notebook and scanned the top sheet. "We have three teachers, Morton, Sylva, and Reeder. They each have one student to discuss. I figure we'll be out of here in about an hour."

Riley took another sip of his coffee. "We will need one less chair," he said when he put his cup down. "I got a call from the county co-op this morning. Elaine Simmons has been re-assigned full time to the largest school in the county. She won't be our school psychologist anymore."

"She what?" Leonard said trying not to betray his complete surprise. "Why? What for?"

"They didn't say," Riley shrugged.

"Is it permanent? Did she request a transfer?" This time the questions came without a disguised calm.

"Your guess is as good as mine. You know what it's like. The number one rule in education is that the bureaucracy must be served." Riley sensed more in the questions than was being spoken. "She may be returned to us next week. Who knows! No one can figure those guys out down there."

Leonard opened his file folder of papers and pretended to read. Had she done this herself? Had he driven her away? Maybe they could have worked things out. Maybe there was still a chance. Maybe it was for the best. Maybe he was thinking crazy thoughts and this was fate's way of telling him to come back to reality.

The door opened and the other members of the team came in talking about some reality show they had watched last night. "He should be voted off," one of them said. "You can't trust him."

As expected, the meeting lasted about an hour. But Leonard hardly said a word. He went home directly after the meeting and finished most of a six-pack. It was well past midnight when he finally put down his book and went to bed. He spent the night in a confused, fitful sleep.

⊶

The team sat quietly on the gym bleachers. In a few moments, they would go out on the field to play the second game of the season. There was an occasional nervous cough and quiet whisper, but otherwise it was completely silent. Music from the Karo marching band wove its way through the open windows at the top of the gym. The loudspeaker was giving information about the Future Farmers of America chili feed in the concession stand. Occasionally some words could be heard distinctly, but most of the time it was muted garble.

The tension in the bleachers was obvious on the faces of all the young men. They would soon cross the parking lot, over the practice field and kneel in the end zone for the announcement of the starters. The memory of last week's embarrassment hung in the air.

Leonard couldn't remember the last time he had been so nervous. How would they do?" What if they fell apart again? He looked over at William standing calmly by the door. He didn't seem nervous at all. "I guess when you've been in a war," Leonard thought, "a football game was nothing to get excited about."

"Okay men," Leonard said quietly, "let me have your attention." All eyes turned toward him. He saw more than one blank stare coming back. They were not as good as he at disguising their uneasiness.

"On offense, we're going to have Brad call the plays. Everyone look to him. He will either call you to a huddle, or call the play at the line of scrimmage. The live color will be red, so if you hear any other color, ignore the play change. Greg will give the offensive line calls,"

Leonard took a deep breath. "On defense, Josh will give the linebacker calls, Alan will give the line slants, and Jason will give the secondary its rotation. Jason and Brad will be captains for tonight, so they will make the decisions on penalties."

There was a short pause. "What about you, coach?" Jason asked.

"Coach Roundtree and I will advise if we see something we think might help, but otherwise we're turning the game over to you."

This time the pause was longer. "Coach," Josh's voice sounded more than a little confused. "You mean that we are going to run the game ourselves? I've never played a game where the coach didn't tell me what to do. I don't know if it will work."

"It will work," Leonard said calmly. "Look," he said evenly, "this game isn't about who has the better coach. It is a contest of one team against another. This is your team. You own it. It's about time you took that ownership."

There was more silence. The muffled sound of the loudspeakers drifted through the windows again. But the silence didn't last very long. In the neighboring locker room there rose the voices of the Canton High players as they began yelling and whooping themselves into a frenzy. Their war cries drowned out the speakers for a moment, and everyone on the bleachers followed the voices of the visiting team as they filed out of their door chanting, shouting, and yelling encouragement to each other.

For an instant, Leonard saw his team was afraid. The howls and cries of their opponent had slapped them across the face and told them to shrink back into their shell. It reminded them of who they were. They were the Karo Eagles. They were the worst team in the state. How dare they even think otherwise.

"You don't get any points for making noise," Leonard said. But the fear in the air still enveloped everyone. Most of them looked like they were already beaten.

"This game has already begun," Leonard said. "The battle of wills has been joined, and some of us have been jolted by its intensity. But we know what to do," Leonard said enthusiastically. "And when we walk out this door, we will focus on the moment. We will concentrate on what we have learned and disregard the past. We will ignore the distractions and just swim the next wave."

Leonard looked around and saw the team nodding in agreement. "We are a new team," he said. "The past does not apply. Let's go out there and show everyone what kind of team we are, and when the game is over, no matter the result, let's hear everyone say, 'they sure know how to play the game, and they never, ever quit.'"

Now the Karo Eagles let loose with a chorus of shouts and whoops as they filed out the door and jogged toward the end zone.

⸻

Brad came up to the line of scrimmage and surveyed the defense. Canton had gone back to their split four alignment with a three deep zone. The 5-2 they had run for most of the game had been very effective, but now they were giving him their change-up defense. Brad counted the number in the box. Four down and four linebackers. They were stacked against the run. The red call was gone, and the white call was protected by the two outside linebackers. The option outside would be a good call. If he could isolate the strong-side backer he could option the end. The corner would try to come up for support, but he wouldn't be able to let his receiver running free. Option it was.

"18 blue," Brad called to the left and then repeated to the right. He paused for a moment to let the offensive line make their calls. Greg called out the blocking pattern. "Charlie, you!" he shouted. A chorus of dummy calls followed. "I've got rip backer!" Alan called. "No load!" shouted Josh. "Rasputin!" Greg finished. Brad made a mental note to talk to Greg about his calls.

There was a slight hesitation before Brad began his cadence. Out of the corner of his eye he saw the play-side end stepping down to an eagle position. That probably signaled a blitz. He had better be ready to pitch the ball immediately after the mesh.

"Hike! Hike! The ball was snapped. Brad pivoted on his right foot showing the ball to Josh who doubled over it to fake a carry. On his second step Josh veered away from the play side as a decoy. Before he took his third step, the weak-side linebacker met him in the hole with a strong tackle. There was no ball there, but it was a good tackle all the same.

Brad had already done a 180 degree turn by this time and was heading parallel to the line of scrimmage. The veer back was in his peripheral vision rushing for the inside leg of the tackle. They would mesh there for the second fake. Brad could see his pre-snap guess was right. The play-side end was crashing toward the mesh, so Brad used what little time he had for a fake. The veer back was tackled the instant he hit the hole. Brad knew he had to pitch the ball now before he got into the traffic jam. He stepped back, looked for Jason, and pitched the ball to him.

It was a good thing he did because, undetected, the play-side backer had come on a blitz as well, and he was zeroed in on Brad. Canton had taken a chance and sent both backers. It was a gutsy call. Sometimes teams get lucky and throw the ball carrier for a big loss. But sometimes they guess wrong and the result is a big gain.

The Canton linebacker crashed into Brad. In an instant Brad saw the field come up to meet him. He felt the grass brush up against his nose. The Canton player had crunched him, and for a moment Brad couldn't breathe. He rolled over on his back trying to catch his breath. The linebacker above him raised his head and looked downfield. There was a roar from the Karo crowd. "Shit!" Brad heard him say. Now the Canton player rose to one knee and continued looking downfield. "Shit!" he said again.

Brad still couldn't breathe very well, but he propped himself on one elbow and looked downfield as well. Jason was racing down the sideline alone. The corner had done exactly what Brad expected him to do, and played against a pass. The only one left to make the tackle was the safety, and he was ten yards behind Jason.

Brad looked at the pile of bodies around him. He felt he was surveying the aftermath of a multi-car pile-up at an unmarked intersection. "This is the result," he thought, "when people ignore Newton's law that no two objects can occupy the same space at the same time." Suddenly his soreness left him, and Brad began jumping up and down as he headed to the sideline.

The touchdown and conversion brought Karo within four points of Canton with a little over three minutes to play. Twenty-six to twenty-two. If they could just get the ball back one more time. Maybe they could on-side kick and get the ball again. Or they could kick the ball deep and hope to hold Canton to three plays and a punt. If they did that they would have about a minute and a half with the ball.

"On-side kick?" Brad asked Coach Davis.

"The odds of recovering an on-side kick are about 10 to 1 against you," Leonard said, "but I'll let you decide."

The team huddled together. It was decided. They would take the long shot. There were shouts of excitement as the team sprinted out on the field. They could taste it. This was the game. The four dozen fans behind them were all standing.

The on-side kick was a failure. Canton took advantage of the field position and gained two first-downs to ice the game. They kicked a field goal as time ran out. The Eagles lost again by a final score of 29-22.

Leonard shook hands with the opposing coaches and players. His guys were hanging their heads. The longest losing streak in the state had just added another game. Leonard didn't know which felt worse, being blown out the week before, or losing a close one this week. But he was proud of the team. They had put their best effort into the contest. They had given everything they had, they just came up a little bit short.

The team walked slowly toward the gym. "Where the hell did you learn to coach?" someone shouted from the stands.

“Too tired to move?” William asked as he approached the bench. Alan Burns looked up and wiped the sweat from his forehead. It immediately beaded again as if it had never been touched. Everybody else was already in the showers, but Alan had stayed out by the practice field. His breathing was shallow, and his head was low.

“No, Coach. I’m just thinking about something.”

William sat down beside him. “Must be something important,” he said softly. “You seem to be lost in another world.”

Alan brought his head up and wiped his forehead again. It immediately sweated over. “It’s my dad,” he said with a sigh.

William found himself clenching both of his hands into fists. “What did he do?” William asked. He knew the answer would not be good.

“He says I have to quit the football team.” Alan answered and lowered his head again. “I’ve been able to stall him for a while, but he hasn’t forgotten, and the next time….” Alan’s voice faded away.

William had to struggle to contain himself, his anger was so immediately intense. How could a father do such a thing? Again, Sinclair Burns was finding a way to keep his son from having success.

Alan suddenly stood. “Why did I think playing football would change anything?” he asked. “Let’s face it! Everyone knew this would happen. My mom’s an idiot, my brother’s in prison, my dad’s the town drunk, and I’m just another Burns!”

"That's not true," William said.

"Don't you think I know when everyone sees me, they see my dad?" Alan turned on William with a sudden fury. "Don't you know that everyone says I'm going to end up just like him? They're right. I'm just a loser." Alan began to walk away.

William sprang from his seat, grabbed Alan by the shoulders and whirled him around. "Look at me!" he commanded, but the command was not obeyed. "Look at me!" he said again, this time shaking both shoulders in his massive hands. Alan slowly raised his head. Tears were beginning to form around his eyes.

"You are not your father," William said in a much quieter tone. "One day you will leave Karo, and you'll make a life of your own. And it will be a life you can be proud of." William softened his tone even more, but did not loosen his grip.

Alan wiped a tear and looked William straight in the eye. "All my life I've been told I'm stupid, I'm lazy, and I'll never amount to anything," Alan said through short breaths. "He hates me and he doesn't care if I live or die."

"I know," William said slowly and released his grip from Alan's shoulders. "I'm not going to say I know how you feel, because I don't. But I know about your father," William paused, "because at one time I was a lot like him."

Alan looked at William with a confused look. "You're nothing like my father," he said quickly.

"Let me tell you," William said slowly. "When I first came back from Nam, I found it hard to adjust. Most people paid me little mind, and most of those who did were critical of what I had done. I remember I took this English Composition course at Wichita State. There was this lady professor who gave an assignment to write an essay about ourselves. My essay was full of anger; anger about the war, anger about seeing my friends die, anger about the government, nothing but complete anger. I poured by heart and soul into it. I don't even remember the grade I got. The only thing I remember about it was at the end, she had written one comment. "I know how you feel."

William paused for a moment. "Can you imagine? She wrote, 'I know how you feel'." I wanted to ask her, 'have you ever walked into a field of battle and heard the devil laughing over your shoulder? Have you ever killed a man and watched the exact second when his soul left his eyes?' There's no way she could understand me and what I'd been through, and yet she had the vanity to say she did."

William led the two of them back to the bench. "Something in me snapped. I began to hit the bottle really hard. I couldn't sleep, I wasn't eating right, I became a recluse, living and breathing for the moment. In my isolation, my anger grew. I was abusive and I took it out on everyone I came in contact with." William paused and folded his arms in front of him. "My demons were consuming me. I can't tell you the number of times I had my 38 on my lap, just waiting for the right moment to eat a bullet." He looked directly at Alan. "I was just like your father, hating the world and everyone in it."

Alan wiped his cheek but did not respond. For a moment they both sat silently.

"Every man his demons," William said softly. "Some never overcome them. I don't believe I would have either if I had not met Samantha. She saved my life. One time she told me that she wouldn't see me anymore if I didn't stop drinking. I said something like, 'I have to drink, or I will destroy. I'll destroy things, I'll destroy people, I'll destroy myself. It won't matter, I'll just destroy.' Then she said something I will always remember, something I still think about today. She said, 'you really have only two choices in life, you can hate, or you can forgive, and only forgiveness brings hope."

"Does my dad hate me?" Alan asked.

"No," William answered and returned his hand to Alan's shoulder. "No, he doesn't hate you. His anger drives him because that's all he knows. He has chosen not to forgive, so he lives without hope. But you are not your father. You do not have to follow his path."

Alan sat silently for a long time. "Thanks, coach." He finally said. "If I could only get away from there."

"You will," William said. "After this year, you will be eighteen. One more year. You will."

"Do I have to quit the team?" Alan asked.

"The next time he brings it up," William said, "tell your dad you talked to the coach about it, and the coach said you should remain on the team. Tell him that if he wants to talk with us about it, he should contact the coaches."

"Maybe he'll forget about this whole thing until the season is over," Alan said.

"Maybe," William said. "Don't bring it up. Lay low. One year. All you have to do is get through one year."

"Then I can be on my own," Alan said with determination. "Then I don't have to stay in his place. I can go out and make my own way."

William nodded his approval. "That's the way it should be," he said. "That's the way it should be."

"Thanks, coach," Alan said. "I guess I better get inside and hit the showers," he finally added.

"Let's both go in," William said. "No sense sitting out in the sun when you don't have to."

⊂⊃

"Follow me!" Coach Davis called to everybody as he started a slow jog from the practice field toward the school building. The unspoken question of every member of the team was "what now?" They made a quick turn around the gym and headed down the side of the building toward the faculty parking lot. There were only a few cars left in the lot this late after school, but coach Davis steered the team straight toward one of them.

A stray complaint came from the back of the pack, and coach Roundtree reacted quickly. "Let's get going," he said. "If I want to see athletes whine and cry," he called to nobody in particular, "I'll watch sports on T.V."

Leonard finally stopped at a vehicle in the back of the lot. "Over here!" he called. "Everybody gather up here," Leonard instructed as he waved the team over. The players quickly formed in a group and just as quickly quieted when Leonard raised his hand.

Coach Davis walked over to the driver's door of a twenty year old, economy pick-up. Rust spots and an occasional dent clearly showed that it had seen better days. The window was down and the keys were probably under the seat. Such was life in Karo.

"Today we're going to learn what it means to be a team," Leonard said over the wind. "So far this season, we have been individuals, and individuals can never accomplish what a team can. But we won't become a team until we believe in something greater than ourselves. Some of you have yet to realize this. Some of you think that you can be part of the team and still do what you want. Some of you look after yourself first. We must learn to be more than just a collection of individuals."

Leonard paused and let the incessant wind carry away his last words. He turned and patted the roof of the pick-up truck beside him. "This is a nice late model with slight body damage," he paused for a few chuckles. "It belongs to our beloved principal, Mr. Riley Stewart. It has almost 200,000 miles on it and is in desperate need of a new clutch. It has four different shades of red because it has been sitting out in the weather for over twenty years."

"It's still nicer than your car," Brad interjected to a roar of laughter.

Leonard continued through his own laughter. "It is five feet five inches tall, thirteen feet long, and weighs approximately 2,600 pounds." With that, Leonard stepped away from the pick-up, and walked towards the team.

"Jason," he called over the wind, "come here."

Jason walked hesitantly over to his coach.

Coach Davis pointed at the pick-up. "Jason," he said without smiling, "I want you to pick up Mr. Stewart's truck and put it over there in the shade of those two trees."

Jason looked over where coach Davis was pointing. Ten feet away were a couple of seedless Cottonwoods which had been planted by the Karo High School Future Farmers of America a decade ago. They stood swaying slightly in the wind. Jason turned and stared back at his coach. "That's bullshit," he said.

"No," Leonard answered immediately. "Bullshit is not believing in something greater than yourself. Bullshit s thinking that the individual is more important than the team."

"But..." Jason stammered. "I can't do it."

"You will need help," Leonard nodded, "but it can be done if your teammates give you some help." Leonard paused. "Everybody in the world needs help," he said. "It's how things get done."

Leonard paused and let the wind carry his words. "Nobody could do it alone, but a team can. A team that works together for one purpose becomes a unique living body greater that its parts. You must give yourself to the team. If you do this you can accomplish great things."

"There are 17 of you on this team," Leonard said. "Let's see what we can do together."

There was another short pause. "Everybody get around the pick-up." Leonard commanded and slowly every member of the team gathered around it, awaiting instructions. "For a few moments," Leonard continued, "we will cease being individuals. We will become a single unit operating with one will and one purpose. We will become a living entity, and we will carry Mr. Stewart's truck from here to those shade trees over there."

Nobody said anything. Their coach was doing some more crazy stuff. They had come to expect it.

"Be sure to use your legs when you lift," Leonard shouted. "And I want everyone to lift together and step together. Everybody must lift at the same time, and everybody must step at the same time. Does everybody understand?"

There were shouts of agreement. "Make sure you don't let your team members down," he added. "Give your best effort." There was another short pause as the hot wind blew across their faces.

"Okay," Leonard shouted, "everyone get a good grip." He paused until he saw everyone was ready. "On three," he shouted. There was one more pause before Leonard started counting. "One—two—three!" he shouted. The pick-up rose slowly but steadily until it came to rest about knee high with everybody standing around it. There were a few moans from the effort, but the truck was securely in their possession.

"Start with your left," Leonard called, "and head toward the shade trees." He didn't hesitate and called the cadence loudly. "Left, right, left, right! Stay together! Don't be in a hurry! Left, right, left, right!"

Ten steps later they were in the shade of the trees. "Don't put it down yet," Leonard called. "Turn the front toward me," he shouted, "and bring the bed away," The truck began a slow pirouette. "Now," Leonard shouted, "walk it straight back the way you have it." There was a little hesitation, but that was quickly followed by some snickers. "There!" Leonard shouted. "Right there! That's where I want it! Now on the count of three, use your legs and lower the truck to the ground." Leonard could see they were eager to unload their burden. "One, two, three!"

The truck was lowered much quicker than it was lifted, and when it finally sat with all four tires on the ground, there were sighs and moans of relief. Then there were other sounds. Shouts of laughter erupted spontaneously from the group. Team members leaned on each other and began to point and laugh while they were gasping for breath.

"Perfect," Leonard said as he spread his arms wide. "Just perfect," he repeated as he surveyed their accomplishment. He began his own belly laugh. They had put Riley's truck between the two trees all right. The first tree was about two feet from the front bumper, and the other tree was less than a foot from the rear bumper. It was sandwiched in.

"Best job of parallel parking I have ever seen," Josh shouted. "Mr. Stewart's going to need a chainsaw to get home tonight," Brad added.

"Practice is over," Leonard shouted. "Everybody hit the showers." The shouting and laughter continued as the team began to jog back across the parking lot to the locker room. Jason stood for a minute looking at the comical sight before him.

"Everybody in the world needs help," Leonard said as he walked by. "It's how things get done."

⊶

Leonard paced back and forth. The team sat nervously on the bleachers in front of him. It was almost kickoff for the third game. It was another home game. The schedule usually wouldn't open that way, but that meant that the next three games would be on the road. The silence was only interrupted by the occasional quiet cough or whisper. The sound of the Karo band came through the open windows.

Leonard had come to regard this as the hardest part of the game day, waiting the last five minutes before taking the field. He had never been much of a rah-rah kind of guy. How could he pretend to suddenly become one? What could he say to them that they hadn't already heard? There was no magic phrase, no motto, no silver bullet that would inspire them to victory. If it existed, he didn't know it.

Leonard looked to his right near the door and saw William standing as he always did, arms folded, and expressionless. Leonard walked over to him.

"I'm coming up blank," he said. "You want to talk to them?"

William nodded but said nothing, then he slowly made his way to the front of the bleachers. The fidgeting and whispering stopped. For the longest moment, William said nothing. He just stood there with the same expressionless face.

"My ancestors would look at this time before battle as a time of celebration," he began. "There would be dances and feasts as they prepared to engage the enemy. It would be a celebration, but not a party. They knew the seriousness of the day. But still they rejoiced. They sang and danced their joy."

"But they did not try to soothe each other with words like "everything will be all right," or "nothing will happen to you, or "you will be safe." They would tell each other, "it is a good day to die." What they meant was they would fight until they had no life left. It was a pact, a contract that each of them knew the other would honor. Life was so sweet that they would be consumed by it until it was gone. To be a warrior was to taste life at its fullest. To experience the joy of battle was to be completely alive."

William paused again but his expression remained the same. "Do you realize what a privilege this is? Do you know the joy you can receive from this? How many times in your life do you get the chance to celebrate in such a way? How many times do you get to experience life with a heart full of joy? How many times can you say to yourself 'I know what it is like to be fully alive. I know what it is like to fully test myself."

"Perhaps one day you will be working in an office, and you'll stop to think about the times when you were a part of this football team. And as you look out your sealed, air conditioned window, you will recall the joy of these games. You will recall the life surging through you, and you will recall how you put yourself to the test."

"Celebrate these times because they are so few in life. Dance and sing that you have this opportunity. Do not be afraid of the battle. Do not hesitate. Step out and embrace it. Take it fully into your heart. Become a warrior. Forget the final score. Forget if you win the game or not. Enter the arena and put yourself to the test. Then, when you walk off that field, you will celebrate again. You will celebrate that short time where you could grasp life by the throat and understand what it means to say, 'it is a good day to die."

William turned toward the door, and then stopped. He turned to the team once more. "When they left the celebration and went off to battle," William added, "my ancestors would chant 'Hahn-ah-Hah-we-ha' because they knew it was true. "Hahn-ah-Hah-we-ha." "We are one, we are strong"

William turned again and walked to the gym door that led out to the field. Behind him he heard a low murmur. The murmur quickly became a crescendo of whoops and whelps. In an instant the team was filing out the door, their shouts piercing the air. Leonard watched as the last player sprinted out toward the field. He looked at William. He couldn't help himself. He too let out a whoop as the two of them followed the team out to the field.

Brad ran over to confer with the coaches during the change of goals at the intermission between the third and fourth quarter. His breath was shallow, but Leonard could detect no nervousness in his voice, just exhaustion.

"I think their free safety is cheating on his alignment," Brad said as he took off his helmet and took a long drink. "They put him in a middle third rotation, but he rolls up to play contain on the snap. I think we can play action against him and throw into his zone."

Leonard shook his head in agreement. "Tell Josh to decoy his block for a second, and then do a post," he said.

"Coach," Alan jogged up to William panting. William put his arm on Alan's shoulder and pulled him closer. "What is it?" he queried.

"I can't get to their backer. Every time I go out to where he is in his alignment, he's already a step ahead. I end up chasing him and watching him make the tackle. I don't know what to do."

"He's not a barrel, Alan." William looked to his side and saw Ilir with his arms open to the perfect size of a barrel. Alan glared at Ilir like he was a bug at a picnic.

William suppressed a smile. "Look," he caught Alan's attention, "what defense are they in?"

"Fifty-two monster."

"And what's the read of the play side backer in a fifty-two?"

"He will probably key the fullback."

"And?"

"If the fullback comes his side," Alan answered without hesitation, "he steps up to fill the "A" gap. If the fullback goes weak side, the linebacker will scrape and look for the counter."

"So you know where he is going to go because you know where our fullback is going to go. Use that to your advantage. Be a step ahead of him. Out think him. Determine where he will be, not where he is. Cut your angle down and beat him to that spot."

Alan shook his head in agreement. "I'll be waiting for him," he said with a grin. He cast a scowl at Ilir who submissively shrugged his shoulders. The whistle blew and the teams were called back on the field. The water bottles were dropped and the players sprinted back on the field. It was a tie game going into the last quarter, and Karo had the ball.

"No fumbles," Leonard called after them.

The Monroe High players were frustrated. They could feel the game beginning to slip away. This was not what they had expected. They had run out to a two touchdown lead in the first quarter because of a couple of turnovers, and knew that Karo would lose heart. Karo would follow the age old formula of the loser, get behind, lose confidence, and quit. They knew there was nothing more disheartening to a team with no confidence than to get behind early in the game. Karo would fold. They always had in the past. They would do so again.

But this time something was different. Even when they were behind, Karo didn't stop fighting. In fact, they had tied it up by halftime and now they were threatening to take the lead. Only another fumble had prevented them from putting a third touchdown on the board. The Monroe players could feel it. This was not a Karo team of the past.

The official blew the ready for play whistle and Brad brought the team up to the line of scrimmage. The defense was showing the same fifty-two monster to the strong side. They were three deep, but they rotated to two deep and brought both the strong safety and the weak safety up for support. How had he missed that before? They had been doing that for most of the second half. It was a good disguise, and they had fooled Brad the past three drives. "I got you now," Brad thought. "I didn't get a 33 on my A.C.T. for nothing."

"18 Go!" Brad called to both sides. "18 Go!"

"I got one alone," Alan gave the line call. It was followed immediately by the other linemen calls. "Charlie you! Tom! Napoleon!

Again, Brad made a mental note to talk to Greg about his dummy calls.

The play began like every other option he had run all night. The fullback mesh and release, the pivot and the 180 degree turn. The inside veer fake to the back and the option back trailing. They had run the same play dozens of times. Only this time, Brad broke from the option and dropped three steps to pass. Sure enough, the free safety had read the option and had come up for support while the strong safety was playing contain in the flats. If Jason could just get inside position on the corner, the pass would be there.

And it was. The ball fluttered as much as it spiraled, and Jason had to slow down several steps to catch it, but he was clearly open. The crowd roared approval as he raced into the end zone followed by several very frustrated Monroe defenders.

Brad jumped up and down. They had these guys. He could see it in their eyes. The willpower of the other side had just broken. The toughest part of the game was over. Coach had been right. In every game there was a point where the clash of wills determined who would win. Karo had forced their will on their opponent. This was their game. This was the game to break the streak. They were no longer losers.

Karo scored another touchdown six minutes later when Jason broke free on a fullback trap for forty-seven yards for the final score of the game. The last five minutes were surreal for the Karo bench. Five years of frustration was coming to an end. The streak was over. It would be a day the players would remember for the rest of their lives. When the final horn sounded ending the game, the score on the board showed Home 28, and Visitors 14.

Leonard wanted to jump up and down as the final seconds ticked off the clock. Instead he turned to William and gave him a big hug. The streak was finally over. He made his way across the field to shake hands with the opposing coach. The other coach took his hand and congratulated

Leonard while he was biting his lower lip. Leonard felt hands clapping him on the back. Handshakes came out of nowhere. One of a dozen hugs knocked his cap off.

When Leonard rose back up from getting the cap, he suddenly saw Elaine. She was laughing with a group not far away. She had come to the game! Leonard didn't know if he was more excited about breaking the losing streak or having Elaine there to see it. God she was gorgeous. He suddenly got those feelings again. He had to go talk to her.

Then two things happened simultaneously. Leonard was immediately surrounded by a group of well-wishers, and Elaine turned to talk with some man Leonard didn't know. The man put his arm around her waist and pulled her to his side. She leaned in to say something to him, and Leonard lost his view. The crowd of well-wishers and parents surrounding Leonard each wanted to congratulate and share their joy with him. Leonard tried unsuccessfully to glance over them as he made small talk, but it was no use. He couldn't escape. There were too many of them.

Leonard said all the right things, gave credit to the team, thanked William and hoped it would not be the only victory of the season. It seemed like hours while the group kept him captive, but it was only minutes. When they finally broke away and left him alone, Elaine and the man were gone.

Leonard looked toward the parking lot and saw Elaine walking with the stranger toward the exit gates. He jogged quickly after them. Then they, too, were stopped by another couple and began talking with them. What would he say? Had anything changed? Before he knew it, he was tapping Elaine on the shoulder.

"I'm glad you came," he said when she turned around. Her eyes showed a genuine pleasure in seeing him, and her smile radiated the joy of the moment.

"Congratulations!" she said as she gave him a quick hug. "You should be very proud." Leonard searched her eyes, while thinking of something to say.

"Colin." A hand reached out simultaneously with the announcement of the name. "Colin Alexander." Leonard broke his gaze with Elaine and took the hand. The man offering it was a handsome specimen in his mid-thirties, dressed in a hundred dollar shirt with a two-hundred dollar sweater tied by the sleeves and hanging behind his neck. He had a full head of hair, straight white teeth, and the scent of expensive cologne. Leonard felt a lump in his throat.

"Strong grip," Colin said, "reminds me of the mechanic who works on my Lexus."

"I'm so glad I talked Colin into coming to the game tonight," Elaine interrupted. "I'm so happy the team won!"

"Yes," Colin added, "it was marvelous to see you guys finally win one after fifty-three, was it fifty-three?"

"Fifty four," Leonard corrected.

"Let's hope it's not another fifty-four before you win again," Colin said. Leonard saw a smile that was both sarcastic and honest at the same time.

Colin broke the handshake and immediately put his arm around Elaine's shoulders. "This is my competition?" Colin thought as he continued to look at Leonard. "This is the man she was telling me about? There was no malice in his gaze, just contempt. "How could he be compared to me?"

Leonard didn't know what to say. He felt numb.

"We really, can't stay too long," Colin said to Elaine. "It's a forty-five minute trip back to Wichita."

"I know," Elaine nodded and reached out both hands to Leonard. He took them but didn't feel them. "I really am happy for you," she said. Her voice was sincere, and her eyes were full of joy.

"Thanks," Leonard managed to push the sound out despite the lump in his throat. He watched them walk away. He watched as Colin's arm pulled Elaine close and they walked out the gate to the parking lot.

Leonard closed his eyes. What had he done? Was he completely stupid? It was over. He had reached bottom. He might as well get a lobotomy and watch a lot of television.

He felt a hand patting him on the shoulder. He heard Riley's voice. "This is probably the biggest win in the school's history," he said, "and you look like you just had a full rectal exam."

"You always were tactful," Leonard said in a distant voice.

"What's wrong," Riley asked and then turned to see what Leonard was looking at. It was easy to interpret what he saw. He was not surprised. Elaine was a beautiful woman inside and out. Riley sought to change the subject. "You've done a fine job," he said catching Leonard's eyes again, "better than anyone expected."

"Thanks," Leonard said, "but the team did all the work. I just went along for the ride."

"That may wash with others," Riley chided, "but don't try to sell it to me. The team looked better this game than they have in ten years." Riley paused. He could sense he had lost his partner in this conversation. "Tell you what," Riley clapped Leonard on the shoulder again, "why don't you come over to the house," he said. "We'll make Pete Coors a little richer."

Leonard stared out at the gate one more time. "Nah," he said shaking his head. "I think I'll just go on home."

"Are you sure," Riley asked. "Are you all right?"

"I'm fine," Leonard gave the predictable response. "I just have to live in the real world."

Before Riley could ask about that statement, a new wave of well-wishers surrounded both of them. Again the litany of congratulations of a job well done cascaded over Leonard. But he only heard part of it. After a short while, he excused himself and went to the locker room. Being with the team raised his spirits considerably.

An hour after the last player had left the locker room, Leonard opened the door to his house. He shuffled from quiet room to quiet room. Perhaps he should read. He decided not to. He put an anthology of his favorite arias on the compact disk player and sat on the couch drinking a beer. He heard the occasional beeping of horns, shouts, and radios blasting through the night air. Karo would celebrate tonight.

He had a lot to celebrate tonight as well. He had successfully defended his way of life. He had protected his routines. He had turned back the scourge of a second chance. He had hardened his heart.

Leonard finished his beer and went to sleep on the couch. He stumbled when he finally went to bed at three o'clock.

William and Leonard sat in the shade of the many elms surrounding the Roundtree home. "Don't you remember?" Leonard asked. "Five years ago, you almost lost every one of these trees to Dutch Elm disease. I remember you working to save them and nurse them back to health. I remember remarking to Linda how wondrous it was to watch you put in the hours you did to save them. And I swear," Leonard stopped puffing on his pipe to add emphasis, "that once I even saw you talking to them. Here was my neighbor, talking to a tree!" Leonard almost laughed with the last sentence.

William said nothing and continued bent over in his lawn chair turning the crank on the homemade ice cream maker. Against the setting sun, he looked like a big brown bear hunched over a honeycomb, knowing that to enjoy the prize within, he must first pay the price.

"I don't know if I would have shown such concern," Leonard added. "I probably would have shrugged my shoulders and cut the trees down."

"Why don't you take a turn at this?" William said finally looking up at Leonard.

"Why don't you get one with an electric motor?" Leonard asked.

"Just like a white man," William answered. "The old ways are never good enough."

Leonard smiled slightly and reached for the crank. "It would save you time and effort," he said.

"Saving time is an illusion," William said without hesitation, "and a man's effort should be embraced."

Leonard's slight smile became broad. He loved these Sunday conversations with William. He put down his pipe, leaned forward in his chair and took the crank handle from his friend. "We'll do it the Indian way," he said through an exaggerated sigh. Leonard made a point to maintain the same continuous, repetitive revolutions that William had used. If it were not turned correctly, the ice cream would freeze unevenly, or all the strawberries would settle to the bottom. They both sat quietly for a moment as the cicada began their eternal song.

"How did we get to be such good friends?" Leonard suddenly asked as he looked up at William. "We appear to be so different. Any outside observer would wonder how it happened."

The question was placed, perhaps, with an element of jest, but it seemed to strike a serious chord with William, who gathered his thoughts for a moment. "Because you understand so much," he answered slowly. "You know why I talked to my trees."

William leaned back in his lawn chair and watched Leonard do the work for awhile. "You know when the white men first came to this land, my ancestors could not really understand them. The whites were stingy with their belongings, but insatiable in their desire to have more of them. They lived from rules put down on some papers, and rarely thought for themselves. They built permanent homes claiming they owned the land. How could anyone own land? That was like owning the air. To the white man, nature was an obstacle to be overcome. It was a commodity. The whites even saw each other as a resource. All in all, my ancestors regarded you guys as humans without a soul. You were like zombies with amazing tools and weapons doing crazy things."

"It's too bad there was never a real understanding between the white world and ours," William continued. "The white world never saw the complexity and genius of our world. Our world was a magical place of talking animals, myths, dreams, and visions. It was a place created by the Great Spirit who we regarded as a spiritual force that was the source of all life throughout the universe. Everything in it, the sun, the animals, and even the trees were examples of this almighty being. In such a world, why would it be impossible to talk to a tree?"

William leaned forward in his chair and took the crank handle back from Leonard. The slow rhythm of the ice around the cylinder never stopped as it made the transition from one man to the other. "You are my friend because you understand such a world. You hold people above things. You hold your spirit above your body. You know that what is important can not be seen."

Leonard leaned back in his chair. He wondered if much had changed in the last 500 years except technology. Was William right? Were most Americans just robots going through their life oblivious to everything around them? The modern world was about acquiring more and more things. No wonder there seemed to be a desperate search for meaning among people. Things did not have a spirit. Things could never love back.

"Now it's my turn," William said and looked up from his cranking. "I put the question to you. How did we get to be such good friends? What would you tell the outside observer?"

Leonard took the question with the same earnestness with which it was placed. "There are only two ways to judge someone," Leonard answered slowly, "by what he says and by what he does. Everything else is just decoration. And I judge you to be strong, humble, selfless, and brave."

There was a short pause. "You'd make a hell of an Indian," William finally said as he stopped turning the crank. "You want me to swear you in?"

"What's involved?" Leonard played along.

"There's a secret ceremony," William said with a smile, "kind of like becoming a Mason."

Their laughter was interrupted by the screen door slamming shut on the back porch. They both turned to see Samantha carrying three bowls with a spoon for each. "What have you two been doing?" she asked as she approached.

"William was about to make me an honorary Indian," Leonard announced.

Samantha handed a bowl to each of them. "Oh really, what tribe?"

"He's not a complete ass," William answered quickly in his usual monotone, "so I was thinking probably a Semihole"

The eruption of laughter probably caused a few neighbors to look out their windows, but it eventually faded. It was a peaceful, relaxing evening, and Leonard forgot about his worries for a while. The ice cream was so good that the three of them ate until it was all gone.

When Leonard finally got home, he was surprised to see a flyer on his front screen. It announced a petition drive was underway. Spearheaded by Christopher and Tiffany Edwards, it called for the undersigned to support closing the Karo public schools and consolidate with the neighboring Silas school district.

There was to be a meeting of all those interested at the Edward's home this Saturday afternoon, and the completed petitions would be taken to the board meeting next month. Leonard wadded it up and threw it in the trash.

That night Leonard had a light, fitful sleep. His dream had two parts. In the first part, he was looking for a job. In the second part, he dreamed he was talking to his trees.

The folding doors closed with their familiar squeak. William read the names of every player from the list, and then sat down to drive the yellow truck disguised as a school bus. It was the first of three away games, and Leonard was not looking forward to it. At least he would get to see some of the fall beauty Kansas had to offer. It was about an hour drive to Southwest High School and the road wound through some of the most beautiful rolling hills in the state. A multi-colored canopy covered parts of the path as they rolled over the narrow two-lane highway.

On the bank of a distant creek, Leonard caught a glimpse of a flock of wild turkeys scurrying to get away from the noise of the bus. Every now and then, the bus would crest a hill, and Leonard would smile at the dozens of colors. On the horizon, he saw a large bank of clouds building in the southwest. He shook his head. If they continued to develop in this direction, they could mean trouble later on during the game.

"Coach!" Leonard turned to see Josh standing by his seat in the middle aisle. The rolling of the bus from side to side like an ocean wave had apparently been enough of an inspiration for Josh to pretend he was surfing. "I'm hanging ten," he said to the chuckles of his teammates.

"Sit down, Josh," Leonard said and waved at him to be seated.

"But I'm just catching the wave!" Josh protested. "I'm..."

"PLANT YOUR BUTT NOW!" William commanded from the driver's seat. Josh planted his butt amidst the laughter of the entire bus.

"Jeez," Josh said to Jason as he plopped down next to him. "What's Roundtree got up his ass?"

"You're really wound up," Jason said. "I don't remember you being so hyped for a game before."

"Lawrence is going to be there tonight," Josh said. He made it sound like an apology.

Jason nodded. He understood. The only perfect carbon-based biped mammal life form to walk the earth, Lawrence Hunter, was going to watch his younger brother try to do things he had already done so much better.

"My dad made a big point of telling me Lawrence was driving all the way down from Topeka, and it would be a big disappointment to him if he came down here, and I had a bad game." Josh looked down at the floor. "He told me the story again about Lawrence throwing three touchdowns against Harrison High with a dislocated left thumb."

"I've heard that one too," Jason nodded again. "He sprained it when he got it stuck up his ass."

Josh laughed at the image, but the laughter quickly died and the rumble of the bus tires below them was all that was heard.

"I try the best I can," Josh said as if Jason weren't there. "I get good grades, I work hard, and I don't get into trouble…" his words faded off. "But no matter what I do, no matter how well I do it, it's never good enough. Mom and dad can always find something I could have, or should have, done better." Josh looked out the window toward the storm clouds in the distance. "My dad has never once said he's proud of me." The words faded quickly into the hum of the tires, and for a while, that was the only sound either heard.

Jason elbowed Josh until he turned around and looked at him again. "In one more year," he said, "you'll be out of there." Jason paused. "I don't think my mom is going to let me leave home next year."

"What about the scholarship you received?" Josh asked. "You're the best player on the team. You may be the best player in the league."

"My mom is always sick," Jason said with resignation. "I have to stay at home to take care of her."

There was another long pause. Finally, Josh leaned back on the seat and closed his eyes to try and rest. Jason did the same.

Leonard took off his cap and wiped his brow with his sleeve. In a few minutes the team would go out of the locker room for the kick-off. He put his cap back on and adjusted it twice. He didn't like wearing caps because he didn't like the feel of them. But he was supposed to wear one because football coaches wore them, and he was a coach. At least he could look like one. He saw William standing by the door with the same stoic expression he always wore before a game. No hat. Leonard dropped his cap to the floor.

"The story of Don Quixote is about an old man who appears to be going crazy," he said to the team. Very quickly all eyes were on him. "His family and friends all come to his rescue, however. They want to help him. They want to save him from his insanity. They are all terribly upset that all those books he was reading had confused him and driven him insane."

Leonard wiped his sleeve over his forehead. "And what was his insanity? What was he doing that was so crazy? Well, first of all, he treated a lowly peasant woman with the respect usually given a noble queen, and he fought injustice wherever he saw it. He did the right thing without any thought of worldly gain. He gave no thought to personal power or wealth. In short, he imagined the world as it should be, and acted as if it were that way."

Leonard paused again. "What does that story say to us? We all know about the real world. We know how things are. We know the good guys don't always win. We know that those who cheat and lie have an advantage over those who don't. We know the powerful usually get their way."

Leonard spoke more forcefully now. "Southwest High has had a winning season for ten straight years. We have won one game in five years. The way things are tells us to accept that as part of the real world, and that we will be beaten soundly tonight. The real world tells us "that's the way it is" and don't' try to fight it, because the Karo Eagles don't have a chance."

"But like Don Quixote, we can step out of the real world. We can think insane thoughts. We can believe that there should be justice, freedom and equality in the world, and that jails should not be the reason why people do the right thing, or that money is the measure of a man. We can even believe that the Karo Eagles will not be judged by their past, but by their accomplishments right now."

"It would be crazy to play this game as winners who hustled and fought hard and gave their best effort. It would be insane to show good sportsmanship without hesitation. It would be shocking if we acted like that poor, insane old man, and played with a determined purpose, like we had a noble cause. People would walk away saying we were crazy. The Karo Eagles were never supposed to win, because that's not the way things are."

Leonard smiled broadly. "But that's exactly what we are going to do," he said. "Let's try it. Let's be good sports because it's the right thing to do. Let's play hard even though we're not expected to. Let's throw out the real world for one evening and let's enter the world as it should be. For one night, let's be noble and brave and gallant. And when the contest is over, win or lose, we will walk off the field with our heads held high."

Leonard said nothing else and walked toward the door. The team quickly followed as coaches Davis and Roundtree led them out on the field amid a chorus of whoops and hollers.

The rain began just after half-time, and it turned what had been a very well played game by both teams into a war of attrition. The first half showcased the two option teams as well prepared and evenly matched. What was developing now was surreal. For a few seconds it would pour, and then unpredictably, it would ease up a little, but throughout the third quarter, the rain had been relentless. The middle of the field looked like a rice paddy, and the players resembled beings akin to Bigfoot.

"Time out!" the official called and waved his arms over his head to stop the clock. "Time out!" he repeated as he pointed both arms toward the Southwest sideline. The officials were the exception among the prehistoric participants on the field. Except for their shoes, they remained clean and mud free.

Leonard waved the team over to the sideline. Everyone was talking at the same time. "They're running a seven man line, with the middle backer protected to every gap," Brad said. "I can't hear the audibles," Greg said. "I got mud up my butt!" Jason muttered. Leonard called them in closer, and they slopped over to surround him.

Leonard raised his hand to stop all the talking. "Guys," he said, "I know there is nothing we can do with our option in this weather. As a matter of fact, we can take our entire game plan and throw it out the window. Playing in these conditions is beyond any plan." As if on cue, the rain suddenly began to fall faster and forced Leonard to shout to be heard.

"This is exactly the time when our intelligence matters most," he said. "Our ability to adapt to this new environment should be our goal. Our new opponent is the weather. You guys are the ones out there. You tell me. Give me your suggestions."

"I suggest we only use our isolation series," Brad shouted over the rain. "Any hand-off is risky, but they are the simplest plays we have."

"But we can't pull or trap on this field," Alan answered, "and we need both to run our isolation plays."

"Then we don't hand off," Jason interjected. "We have our quarterback carry the ball every time."

"How would that work?" Leonard turned to Jason.

"Well," he answered, "in the seven diamond they have a down man assigned to every blocker. All we have to do is pick the gap we want for each play. We can alternate to different gaps."

"And we can alternate quarterbacks," Brad nodded, "that way I won't get completely exhausted."

"How are we going to block at the point of attack?" Alan asked.

"Don't block them," Greg offered. "We'll use an influence block. We'll pull down the line, and if he does what he's supposed to, the defender will follow. He'll take himself out of the play."

"And the backs who are not carrying the ball can fade outside and influence too," Jason said.

"Sounds like a good plan to me," Leonard said. "We'll rotate quarterback every two plays. Brad goes first, then Josh, then Jason, and back to Brad."

"Play ball coach!" Leonard looked over and saw the official waving the team back on to the field. The whistle sounded through the constant pounding of the rain. Leonard suddenly wished he had kept his hat on.

"Just remember," Leonard shouted before the huddle broke, "our new opponent is the weather. Think about that before you make any decision on what to do."

The whistle blew again and the official waved them to the ball. Even though the official was clean, he didn't want to stand in a cold monsoon any longer than he had to. The rain ebbed a bit as the two teams resumed battle. The quagmire in the middle of the field had turned from a rice paddy into a very saturated surface of the moon.

Brad brought the team to the line. The "A" gap was the call. He gave the audible to the line and went under center for the snap. The ball was cold and wet, and he almost lost his grip at the snap, but he gained control and tucked it under his arm. Out of the corner of his eye, he saw Jason and Josh scatter in opposite directions. Just as they suspected, the Southwest linebacker to each side mirrored their movements and headed toward the sidelines.

Brad turned his attention to Alan. He watched him pull out of his stance and slog down the line of scrimmage as if to lead on a sweep. The defender didn't hesitate to follow him, and Brad headed right where he had been. Twelve yards later, the weak side safety pulled Brad down. Brad got up spitting muddy water from his mouth, but he was grinning. It had worked. They had them.

On the next play, Brad gained another ten yards, and they had another first down. Josh gained six and eight. Jason picked up ten yards each time he carried. It didn't seem possible, but the rain increased its intensity. They had trouble hearing the calls. They had trouble keeping their footing. They had trouble holding onto the ball, and they couldn't see more than twenty yards down the field. But they were moving the ball toward the end zone.

Six more yards, then three, and then three more led to another first down. Brad noticed the other team was arguing among themselves. Three yards, five yards, four yards, and another first down. Two more first downs, and the Southwestern Broncos were defending their own goal. It was Josh who carried the ball into the end zone for the touchdown. The conversion failed when Jason slipped as he tried to kick it. If there was any cheering from the crowd, nobody heard it through the rain.

After that drive, Southwestern changed their defense. They abandoned the seven diamond and played a forty-three read. For the remainder of the game neither team could move the ball at all, and the fourth quarter ended with a six point win by the Eagles. The unthinkable had happened. Karo had won two games.

Ilir steadied himself, but found it hard to stand on the stack of towels lying in the bottom of the laundry hamper. "You are sure this is an American custom?" he asked.

"It sure is," Greg answered. He and Brad were in their street clothes, sans shoes.

"Remember when we asked coach if we could run the "Statue of Liberty?" Brad chimed in. "What did coach say."

Ilir puzzled for a moment and then quickly answered. "Coach said that the "Statue of Liberty" was a part of football for many years."

"There you go," Greg said and patted the back of the ninety pound blond beanpole. "He also said that we could run it once this year, and you are privileged to be the one chosen to do it."

Ilir shook his head. "You have many strange American customs," he said.

"Look," Brad said in a serious tone, "everyone in America loves that statue, and when you go out there every girl on the volleyball team will stop what she is doing, look at you, and be reminded of this great country. So you go out there and stand tall and stand proud."

So Ilir stood in all his glory, chin up, chest out and arm extended. He wasn't wearing a shirt, but he had a towel wrapped around his waist and a pair of shorts on underneath for insurance.

"You might even get a few dates out of this," Greg said. "I've seen the way some of those girls look at you."

Ilir immediately turned red, but he was convinced. "I will do it," he said, "for America."

Mrs. Zimmerman was in the corner of the gym working with the setters. She had the rest of the team at the net working on spikes and digs. She didn't notice the commotion at first, but quickly the sound of bouncing balls was replaced by giggles, squeals, and roaring laughter. She turned to see what was going on.

Greg and Brad were pushing a laundry cart around the outside of the volleyball court. Coach Zimmerman's mouth opened, but no sound came out. Riding in the cart with only a towel around his waist, Ilir Kucoj was standing as stiff as a 1950's hood ornament. He was stone faced and oblivious to the reactions around him. A bic lighter glowed in his up stretched hand.

Mrs. Zimmerman stood frozen as they whirled by her. She thought she heard Brad and Greg singing "God Bless America." She still hadn't moved as they went down the other side of the gym, and her mouth was still open when they crossed back over to the boy's locker room and disappeared through the swinging doors. Half her team was rolling on the floor as the other half stood and applauded.

She slowly shook her head. "I knew I should have gone into real estate," she moaned.

Except for the music, and some of the dance moves, the fall dance had not changed much in thirty years. The commons area was decorated with crepe paper and multi-colored streamers lined the walls. The D.J. was blaring out tunes from two ear-blasting amplifiers that would leave everybody's head ringing for days afterward. Some couples arrived late, stayed for the pictures, danced a few times, and then headed off to the real parties where they could have beer. The faculty sponsors stood around and reminisced about the dances of their youth and how their generation had better music.

This was a part of the job that Riley would not miss at all. School dances were a gigantic pain in his backside. He found himself smiling, however, as he realized that this was the last year he would have to go through this. After thirty-five years, he would no longer be obligated to come and watch teenagers go through these frenetic mating rituals. The smile on his face grew wider as the night went on.

Leonard stood next to him trying to figure out the growing smile on Riley's face. Leonard rarely came to these school dances. He usually claimed he was busy, but in reality, he didn't come because he couldn't stand the music. He didn't want "musicians" to scream at him for three hours. He had tried to like it, but he couldn't. Maybe, he thought, he was just getting too old.

Nothing eventful happened during the dance and at midnight it broke up. The two dozen or so who had stayed for the entire evening drifted off to their cars. Some would go directly home, while others would head out to the park. Riley and Leonard stood outside the Gymnasium doors to make sure everyone had a ride home. Leonard looked curiously at his friend. The smile on Riley's face was enormous. He would have to ask him why.

Before he could, however, a car pulled into the parking lot heading straight for them. It was going too fast. It almost screeched to a stop at the curb next to them. Lewis Applegate and his girlfriend, Louisa Cody, got out of the car and walked quickly up the steps.

"Where's the fire," Riley asked as if he were getting ready to give them a lecture on their driving.

"Mr. Stewart," Lewis said about halfway up the stairs, "Josh just had a wreck on county six. He rolled his car. I was taking Louisa home and we saw the car in the ditch."

"How badly was he hurt?" Leonard asked.

"We don't really know," Lewis answered. "When we got there, Josh was walking around the car cussing and muttering to himself. I think he had been drinking. I wanted to call 911 on my cell, but he wouldn't let me. He said he would get his uncle's tractor and pull it out tomorrow."

"Do we need to go out there? Is he still there?" Riley asked.

"No," Louisa answered this time. "We took him home. We didn't know what else to do."

Leonard and Riley were silent for a moment. "Why do you say that you thought he was drinking?" Leonard pressed. "Was he drunk?"

"I don't know," Lewis said. "He was able to walk around and talk to us, but I could smell beer on his breath."

Riley thanked the two of them and then sent them on home. "I'm going to call Josh's house right now," he said when the pair left them. He grabbed his keys and headed for the front door of the school. He hadn't brought his cell, and the school phone was a lot closer than the one at home. He was putting the key into the lock when another car pulled up to the front of the building. It was Bill Grunwald. Bill was probably checking to see if everyone knew about the rollover. Riley went inside and made the call, but the line was busy. He tried twice with no luck.

He came back out just as Mr. Grunwald's truck pulled away. "Now what?" he asked Leonard.

"Now we know why Alan Burns didn't come to the dance tonight," Leonard said in a distant voice. "Bill just said that the county deputy was called out to the Burns' house about an hour ago. There had been a fight. Alan and his dad got into it." There was another long pause. "They can't find Alan anywhere. They think he's run away."

Louis Freeman studied the paper in front of him but couldn't quite make out the figures. He put it down, searched for his glasses and found them next to his coffee cup. He returned to the report. Louis had been with the Wichita plant for over thirty years. He had had opportunities to live in other cities, but he preferred living in Wichita. He found the living easy in a town of half a million people. Living in a large metropolitan area of millions held no attraction for him. Besides, he figured, the bigger cities and Wichita had the same amenities. The bigger cities just had more places doing the same thing.

Louis was one of a handful of black executives at the plant, and now he was in his last year before retirement. A Wichita native, he had earned an engineering degree from Wichita State University, and had taken advanced studies at Stanford. He had always found airplanes fascinating. His two sons were out of the house, married and living with families of their own on the east coast. Sometimes his sister and mother would visit from Florida.

Louis had that rare combination of intelligence and integrity that had brought him to the top levels. Without a dominant ego, he weighed all options and listened to different ideas. He always went with the best idea, even if it wasn't his. Most of the time, however, it was.

"Are you sure the building will be clear a year from now?" he asked.

"The board of education will make the final decision before

Thanksgiving," Christopher Edwards said as he leaned in and handed his boss an eight by ten glossy, "but the district has lost so much enrollment it's almost certain that they will vote to close."

Louis took the photograph from his assistant and looked at it. He wasn't sure how he felt about this new guy, but he was going to reserve his judgment for a while. Although he was a hard worker, Louis couldn't quite get over the feeling that the new junior executive liked to play the angles. Cutting corners, even for the benefit of the company, was something that Louis considered foolish, and cutting corners for personal benefit was something Louis would not tolerate. But he knew what it was like to be judged prematurely, so he would give the new guy every chance to reveal his true self.

Louis put the photograph down and moved his glasses to the end of his nose. "I hate to see that," he said. "We lose a great deal when we lose our small schools," he said and handed the photograph to Christopher.

"Yes, sir." Christopher said without expression.

"I don't think I can make the decision without going on site," Louis said. "The new project will require some very specific accommodations. Whether we buy or build, we must be sure the site has everything we need."

"Building would require at least two year's construction," Christopher interjected, "and another half year to move everything in to get the site ready. We can probably get this," Christopher said pointing to the photograph, "for half the price of new, and be up and running a year from now."

Louis took the photograph back and looked at it again. It certainly did look promising. The size, location, and structure of the property were almost exactly what they were looking for. Time would be a factor as well. If the decision came from the top to get the project going ASAP, there would be enormous time pressure to buy something like this. But still, he hated to se another small school bite the dust.

"I'll take a look at it" Louis finally said. "Check my calendar and set up three different dates. I'll look them over and let you know which day looks the best to me."

"Yes, sir," Christopher said as he gathered up the papers and headed toward the door. "This could be quite a feather in your cap," Christopher said as he opened the door to leave. "You would save the company money and put the project ahead of schedule on one stroke," he said. "And," he added, "it would look great at the end of the year when it came to bonus time."

Louis didn't answer but watched silently as his new assistant exited the room. That last comment was exactly what confused him about the new guy. Louis had been worrying about the fate of the people in that small town, and his assistant saw a huge Christmas bonus. Maybe, Louis thought, he was just getting old. He knew for sure he was getting tired.

"You've got to cover the pitch man on the option play," Brad shouted at Greg. "Linebacker has quarterback and end has pitchman!" Brad did not try to hide his frustration. Nothing was going right for Karo. They were playing on the road in front of a large, hostile crowd, and they were embarrassing themselves. Chisolm High School had just driven sixty-nine yards for another touchdown to end the third quarter ahead 28 to 7.

"They've got a load block on me," Greg countered. "I can't cover the pitchman when I'm tied up with the tight end. Don't yell at me! Talk to the strong safety," Greg shouted back and walked away from Brad.

Leonard could see half the team was just going through the motions. They were arguing among themselves and pointing fingers of blame. They had more penalties this game than the last two combined. It was a flat, uninspired performance, it was what Leonard called playing in "the fog." Once a team was in "the fog," it was almost impossible for them to find their way out of it. The fog enveloped everything, it limited their vision, and it caused fear. It robbed them of their confidence and took away their will. He was seeing signs of the Karo Eagles who had lost 52 straight games.

Jason returned the kickoff out of the end zone, and slipped as he made a cut on the eleven yard line. They had 89 yards to go for a score as they huddled seven yards behind the ball.

"How about somebody doing some blocking this time?" Brad chided.

"How about you don't throw an interception?" Greg retorted.

"I can't do a damn thing because you guys aren't blocking," Brad began.

"Bullshit," Greg interrupted. "You've had blocking, you're just…"

"Enough!" Jason shouted at both of them. "Enough arguing." He held out both arms to signal and end to hostilities. "We're down three touchdowns, but we've still got another quarter to play."

"That won't matter if we keep turning the ball over," Greg quipped while looking at Brad.

"Let's just move on," Jason said ignoring the last statement.

"Good idea," Brad said. "Let's just get through the game."

"Face it," Greg said looking at Jason, "without Josh or Alan, all we can do is try to keep the score close." He looked directly at Brad. "The way some people are playing, we don't have a chance to win."

Brad took a step into the huddle toward Greg. "We win as a team and we lose as a team," he shouted back. Greg took a step toward Brad.

Jason quickly stepped between them. Other teammates pulled them back to their separate places. "What good is all this bullshit?" Jason shouted at them both. "All we're doing is wasting time and energy fighting with each other. Now I don't want anymore of this. We may not win, but we're at least going to try." Jason paused and looked specifically at the two antagonists. "And if you two can't keep your mouth shut, I'll shut them for you."

"Oh, yes sir," Brad answered sarcastically.

"Call the damn play," was Jason's only reply. "Call the damn play."

Brad stared at Jason as if he were thinking of something to say, and then thought better of it. "Right 4, 118 counter," said still looking at Jason. "Ready, break." The team broke the huddle and jogged to the line of scrimmage.

The second after they were in position they were assessed a penalty for delay of game. They had taken too much time in the huddle. Their series went for three plays and ended with a punt. They didn't argue much after that. They just went through the motions. The fog had them in its grip. When the final horn sounded, they had lost 38 to 7. They congratulated the other team and headed to the showers.

"Where the hell did you learn to coach?" Leonard heard from the back of the bleachers as he made his way to the locker room.

The first view of the bridge over the Arkansas River sent a chill down William's back. He was instantly transported back in time, back to another life. In a flash of memory he was lying almost lifeless; a crumpled, broken man, fighting to stay awake on that frosty morning.

He had probably mouthed off to the wrong people in some downtown bar, or maybe he tried to steal something and was caught. It might have been he scammed someone or owed someone money. By whom and for what reason he would probably never know.

They had beaten him and thrown him over the Douglas street bridge, hoping to drop him in the Arkansas River. They must have been drinking too, because their aim was bad, and instead of landing in the river, William fell on the riverbank. A foot to one side and he would have landed on the cement bridge support. A foot the other way, and he would have landed in the water to slowly drown. Either way he would not be alive today.

Another time, another life, William reminded himself. The search for Alan would take him to every spot where the invisible people live. He would check under the bridge later.

William drove slowly past the public library and looked over the heating vents. The vents were always crowded during the colder weather. The homeless would sleep on those giant grates to stay warm from the exhaust. There was nobody there, but it was just barely noon. Perhaps it was too early to stake out a spot. The homeless wouldn't start arriving until sunset.

He parked his car in the convention center lot. He would have to do most of his searching on foot. Alan would be in the shadows, and William would have better luck finding the dark places on foot. To most people, Alan would be in plain sight and still not be noticed. People chose not to look. That way they could feign surprise during the holidays and send a check at Christmas to the Salvation Army. Life was easier when one pretended not to see.

William made a quick search of "old town," the latest development of upscale restaurants, boutiques, and apartments. Somehow he couldn't see Alan sitting in a sports bar drinking a microbrew while watching a game on a big screen television. He left the "old town" section and headed south down Broadway. He didn't have to go far to leave the prosperity behind.

"Hey chief," William turned toward the voice. A gray bearded man covered by at least three overcoats greeted him. "How about a dollar to help with some groceries? I haven't eaten in two days." William knew that any money he handed over would go immediately to the nearest liquor store for a bottle of the cheapest rot gut that could be bought.

William pulled a twenty from his front shirt pocket. He had come prepared. "Tell you what, old timer," he showed the bill and a picture of Alan simultaneously. "If you can tell me where he is, I'll spring for next week's groceries."

An unwashed hand with a pinky finger missing took the picture deftly between his thumb and middle finger. There was no expression of recognition on his face.

"Nah…I…Maybe I seen him…Can't say for sure."

"Listen," William said calmly, "the money is not dependant on you giving the right answer. Just tell me the truth. Have you seen him around?"

The man pushed the Pittsburgh Steelers stocking cap to the back of his head. He seemed relieved to know that he didn't have to guess right to get some money. "There was a bunch of kids round here last night," he said. "I was with Leo and Carl at the Lord's Kitchen for supper and afterward we left and they shared their bottle with me. They call me pinky on account of my right hand don't got no pinky finger." He showed his hand to William as if had not been noticed before.

"I was a roughneck," the man volunteered. "Got the chain wrapped around the pipe and my hand at the same time. Damn near took the entire hand off at the wrist. Ain't nothing easy bout roughneckin. Dangerous too."

Wiliam raised the money into the direct view of the storyteller, and that was enough to cut off the tale before it went further. The appeal of holding a brand new bottle was stronger than the appeal of telling the story. Pinky looked at the picture again. "I can't really tell. It was dark and the kids usually just yell something like "Get a job, Pinky," or "nice haircut, Pinky," shit like that. Mostly the kids sleep around in abandoned buildings during the day and work south Broadway during the night. I don't hardly see any kids during the day."

William traded the picture for the bill. "Tell you what I'm going to do," he said. "I'm going to leave you this picture," he began writing on the back of it. "And I'm putting a phone number on the back. If you see this guy, pick up a phone and call me at this number. Any time, night or day." William put the picture in Pinky's coat pocket.

"Shore," Pinky nodded in agreement as he rolled the twenty dollar bill through his fingers. "Might be if I find him, you could spot me another twenty."

William clapped Pinky on the shoulder. "If you find him, I'll take you out to the best dinner you've had in a year, get you a haircut, and buy you a new set of clothes. How's that for a deal?"

The old man thought for a moment as he rubbed his beard. "I shore could use a new set of clothes for the winter," Pinky said. "And twenty extra would be handy."

"You'll get the cash too," William said as he extended his hand. "Do we have a deal?"

"It's a deal," Pinky said. William was surprised by the strong, confident grip. Pinky's eyes were clear and they flashed the history of a man who once was full of promise, confidence and respect. "In my other world," William thought, "we could have been friends. We could have shared a bottle over stories, watched each other's back, and eventually, watched each other die."

Pinky turned and walked away. William watched him for a long time. Another chill went through him. He could very easily have been the one carrying the new twenty dollar bill quickly to the corner liquor store.

William glanced at his watch and clenched his teeth. He still had two parks to check, the Salvation Army, the Lord's Kitchen, and the police sub-station. He would have to check under the bridges too.

A single desk top lamp illuminated Josh as he sat facing the open window. The breeze blew the curtains around his face as if asking him to play, but Josh was unaware of either the curtains or the breeze. Despite the coolness of the wind, beads of sweat formed on his forehead. He didn't notice them either. He was too intent on his work. It was almost midnight, and the house was silent. His parents were sound asleep. Josh heard the occasional barking from a dog down the block. It was probably Elmer Simon's black lab. She was the nervous type who would bark at shadows. But there were no shadows tonight. Tonight was cloudless and breezy without a hint of moon.

It would have been a perfect night for Halloween, but that was still three days away. Halloween was a good time. Josh could always find a party, get as drunk as he wanted, and get away with it. Best of all, he could be someone else for a night. He had a perfect excuse to not be Josh Hunter. It was almost better than when he was a kid and got candy. Halloween was one of the things he would really miss.

But such thoughts did not stay long in his mind. He was too intent on his work. He wanted to be exact, so he had to be careful. He wanted it to look good. He didn't want any half-assed marks that couldn't be understood. He wanted everyone who saw it to know without hesitation what they were seeing.

Josh swabbed the tip of his pocketknife on the wet paper towel sitting on the window sill. He used the other hand to wipe the blade clean, and satisfied, went back to work. He had been at it for about an hour now. Slice, dab, cut, dab and inspect. Nobody would know. He had a lot of long sleeve shirts.

The breeze carried the sound of the barking retriever softly through the window. The curtains suddenly flapped and then just as suddenly stilled. Slice, dab, cut and inspect. Josh put the knife down and raised his arm into the lamplight for a better look. His brother would be proud. The red, seeping letters L and H appeared on his forearm. They would scar up nicely. Almost done. A little more definition on the "H" and his work would be over.

⊂⁂⊃

The feature for the evening was the "Symphony Fantastique," but Leonard wasn't really looking forward to it. It was a tone poem about a man driven to madness from lost love, who in a fit of passion kills the love he cannot have, and is rewarded with the gallows. Maybe the short Hayden symphony and the opening Coriolon overture would be enough for the afternoon and he could leave at the intermission.

His tickets to the Wichita Symphony were the only luxury he allowed himself. He and Linda had season tickets and so once a month they would make a day of it by having a fine meal at one of the downtown restaurants before coming to the concert. Leonard believed there was not a better orchestra within a five-hundred mile radius of this one. He loved how the music would allow him to forget about everything and take him away from the past, the present, and his life. He could forget for a while.

The Hayden piece was like all others by the composer, soothing in its use of harmony and pace, but the Coriolan was fabulous. Beethoven was truly a titan wrestling with the gods. When the last powerful cords ended, Leonard found himself applauding loudly and, without hesitation, found himself standing with the rest of those in the concert hall showing their appreciation for a job well done.

The lights went up, and Leonard followed the crowd to the lobby. Heading toward the line for a drink, he suddenly stopped in his tracks. Across the lobby stood Elaine. She was radiant. She was with Colin and another man Leonard hadn't seen before. She was dressed in an elegant gown as was the custom for the symphony. Her hair was up and curled. For a few moments, Leonard could not even breathe. He just watched, captivated by her beautiful essence.

What a fool he was. He knew his heart was feeling what he had not allowed it to feel for three years. He could no longer pretend. He had to talk to her and tell her how wrong he had been. He had to apologize and hope she could forgive him. He suddenly had no choice. He had to try again. He could do it. Three years was long enough.

Elaine noticed Leonard halfway across the lobby, and it seemed to him her eyes brightened as he approached.

"Hello," Elaine greeted him while he was still several steps away. Colin and the other man turned from their conversation as Leonard walked up. Colin's face showed mild amusement.

"Hello Elaine," Leonard said quietly but confidently. He extended his hand to Colin. "Good to see you again, Colin."

"Lester, wasn't it?" Colin said with feigned ignorance. Elaine frowned at Colin and made the introductions. "Leonard, you remember Colin, and this is Alex. His fiancée, Rachael, is with us, but she is in the ladies room."

Leonard shook each hand in turn. The awkward silence that usually follows such introductions did not have time to develop. "I'm sorry to interrupt," Leonard said sincerely, "but if you will excuse us, I'd like to borrow Elaine for a moment," he said and offered her his arm.

Elaine did not hesitate or look at Colin. She slowly took Leonard's arm. "Oh...sure," she said and then turned to Colin and Alex. "Will you please excuse me?" she said. Within seconds, Leonard was leading Elaine across the lobby to a quiet corner. The two remaining men were a bit stunned and quietly looked at each other.

"Who the hell is that?" Alex asked when they were out of earshot. "Tell me that's her uncle or something."

"I think," Colin said with a slight sneer, "that is my competition."

"Your competition?" Alex said through a chortle. "You are competing with a fifty year old bad haircut?"

"Elaine is different," Colin said with a sigh, and a hint of respect in his voice. "She's not like anyone else I've dated. She doesn't play games, and she's not impressed by money or position. She said she won't have sex until she's married."

"Jeezus!" Alex almost laughed. "What are you doing with her? You don't have to put up with that."

"I know," Colin nodded agreement.

"I didn't think…" Alex began.

"I know. I know," Colin interrupted and turned his gaze from Elaine to his friend. "All I can say is that Elaine is different, she has different priorities. I'm not used to that. She is a real challenge." For a moment Alex thought Colin revealed some hesitation, even some intimidation.

"What are you going to do?" Alex was genuinely curious now.

"I'm not really sure," Colin said as he watched the conversation between Leonard and Elaine. "But I think I'm gong to raise the stakes. I'm going to be as sweet and supportive as I need to be, and as sincere as I have to be." He turned to Alex and the concern on his face turned into his recognizable sneer. "I'm going to see if I can break this horse."

"If she won't let you play until you pay," Alex whispered, "you will have to convince her of how serious you are."

"I've thought of that," Colin said shaking his head in agreement. "I wonder if she'd change her mind if she were to get a ring." He looked at his friend whose eyes suddenly grew wide. "Don't worry," Colin quickly added, "engagements have been broken before."

Leonard had turned Elaine so he could keep an eye on Colin and Alex while they talked. He didn't want any surprises. "I would like to explain some things to you," he said. "I've was very foolish he last time we were alone. I acted impulsively and I'm sorry."

For an instant Elaine threw up a protective wall. "If you are talking about the time I came to visit you on your porch," she said, "I've already explained that it was a miscommunication."

"No, it wasn't," Leonard cut her off softly but firmly. "You and I both know there is something here that should be explored. Maybe it won't work out and maybe it will, but it deserves our effort. I haven't been able to eat, sleep or work without feeling regret for what I said and did." Leonard softened his tone even more so that he almost spoke in a whisper. "I would like the chance to try again."

Elaine didn't say anything. She was confused and flustered. She took turns looking from Leonard to the floor. "I don't know what to say," she finally answered.

"Say yes," Leonard said quickly. "Let's give us a chance."

Elaine opened her mouth to answer, but they were suddenly joined by Colin and the other couple. Leonard cursed himself for losing track of them. "Hey, you two," Colin said. "Intermission is almost over." As if on cue, the lobby lights flashed off and on again.

"We should get back to our seats," Alex called from behind Colin.

"Yes," Colin agreed and took Elaine by the hand. She offered no resistance and automatically fell in step with him toward the concert hall. Leonard could see great confusion in her face. What was she thinking? If he could only get her alone for a while.

"It was good to see you again," Colin called as the two walked away. "Maybe there are other social circles we both frequent, and we'll meet again."

"Enjoy the concert Uncle Leonard," Alex quipped as he passed.

But Leonard did not enjoy the rest of the concert. In fact, he went home. He had the complete works of Berlioz at home, and he could listen to it there.

Was this day seventy or seventy-one? William couldn't remember. Every night it was the same. Every day it was the same. But they had their orders: hold the ground. Was it seventy days of living in muddy trenches, wearing the same clothes, and sleeping in the rain? Or was it seventy-one? Was it seventy days of dying Marines, rockets and mortars shaking the ground, and sniper bullets whizzing by? Or was it seventy-one?

What year was it? William couldn't remember. Every night was the same. Every day was the same. But they had their orders: hold the ground. Surely, God in His heaven could not allow the living to do these things to each other. It must be a dream. But the moon was not a dream. The earth only had one moon, right? That moon was the same one that rose over Oklahoma, wasn't it? Was this day seventy or seventy-one?

Samantha began shaking William to wake him, and he slowly opened his eyes. These dreams came less often, but they always had William waking up in a cold sweat, rolling from side to side, and talking incoherently. "William," Samantha said softly as she shook him. "William, you're with me. It's Samantha, William. You're with me."

William startled awake and tried to sit up. When he saw Samantha, he instantly relaxed and melted back onto his bed. His breath was shallow and rapid. Beads of sweat covered his body. Samantha laid her head on his chest. "It's okay, baby," she said. "You're with me."

William said nothing. His pulse slowed, his breathing deepened, and his muscles began to relax. This had happened before, and it would happen again. The good Great Spirit had been kind to him and allowed him to come home from the war, but the evil Great Spirit would never let him forget. He closed his eyes and breathed deeply. He would be able to sleep again in a little while. The power of the evil spirit was gone for now. William gave Samantha a gentle hug and a kiss on the forehead.

Samantha made sure that William was sleeping again before she rolled off his shoulder. He would be okay now. The dreams never came twice in one night. But she wondered to herself. What was William talking about? Why did he keep repeating the same numbers, seventy and seventy-one?

⊙═⊰ ⊱═⊙

Leonard tossed again, sat up, and rubbed the sweat from his forehead. He threw the covers back and sat on the edge of the bed. He rose from the bed and walked to the back door to get some fresh air. He opened it a crack. A pale shaft of light from a full moon instantly appeared across the room. A gentle breeze caressed his face. He closed his eyes.

Maybe if he were a younger man. Maybe he would just leave and start over someplace else. When he was a young man he could survive anything. The young have passion and excitement and expectation to fill their days. His days of passion were over, they had disappeared with time.

But when did it happen? When did he trade his passion for comfort? It didn't matter anyway. Life is absurd. You're born, and for the next eighty years you tread water, never going anywhere, never accomplishing anything, and serving no purpose. Eventually when you get tired enough or can't stand the pain anymore, you slip under the surface, leaving no trace that you had ever been there.

Leonard opened his eyes again. He knew why he wouldn't sleep tonight, and it had nothing to do with the school or the team or his age. He couldn't sleep because he was sleeping alone. The one he had loved for the past twenty-seven years was gone, and the one he loved now would never be his.

He knew it now. He loved Elaine Simmons. He felt for her what he had not felt in three years. Elaine made him feel complete. She was the missing part in his struggle to become fulfilled. His years as a member of the walking dead could finally end.

Time spent with her was wonderful. He could be with her, touch her hand, laugh with her, and feel complete again. Time would fly by as if it didn't exist. There was only the moment: a moment with her that led to another moment with her that led to another moment.

He hoped she felt something for him. Perhaps he was just being an old fool. Was she standing in her doorway at this moment staring at the full moon? Did she think of him so much at night she couldn't sleep? Did she ache to hold him? Could she possibly love him?

Leonard closed his eyes again. Life was just a cruel joke. The last few years he had tried to get by on inertia. He wasn't looking for fulfillment or purpose. He just wanted to get through the day. Then Elaine came along.

Nights were hell. Tossing and turning, not sleeping, dream after dream of being with her, laughing with her, making love with her. Leonard could hear the treetops rustle in the breeze. A stray dog barked in the distance. There would be no answers tonight.

A small shiver came over him. How could she love him? She was very, very beautiful. He was very, very average. By the laws of nature and man, beautiful people fell in love with beautiful people. She was out of his league. He could only love her in his heart. She could be a friend who sometimes would give him a quick kiss on the cheek. She could laugh with him and hug him. Maybe they could even have an intimate conversation about love and life. They could even share a tear or two when life was hard.

But she could never love him. He would have to be content to dream of her at night. He would have to pretend the hug of friendship was an embrace of love. He would have to take their moments together and say that it was enough.

But it was not enough. If he could just hold her one time, gently feeling her breath on his chest, smelling her hair, feeling her breasts pressed against him, engulfing her in his arms. If he could just have that moment.

Leonard opened his eyes again. A cloud passed over the moon and the shadows in the backyard disappeared into darkness. Leonard shut the door and walked back to the bedroom. He sat down with his head in his hands. He knew this was his last chance at love, and he knew he would lose it. He would spend the rest of his life loving her at arms length, and aching for her at night.

He might as well go back to his routines. The pain of a life filled with routine was numbing, but the pain of lost love was searing. Leonard laid back down to try to sleep and closed his eyes. They slowly filled with tears.

Silas High School was the biggest rivalry of the season, because both schools were in the same county just twenty miles apart. The students in each school held the same summer jobs, went to each other's prom, and attended the local junior college together after graduation. The farmers from both towns would bitch and moan about the government with the same words when they gathered in the morning in their respective town's coffee shops.

But Silas High School had almost twice the enrollment of Karo, and thanks to a new trailer assembly plant, a new school. The Silas faithful had heard the rumors. The word around both towns was the same. The vote would come within the month. The administration of Silas should prepare to absorb their poor cousins from Karo next year.

The game was nearing the end, and it had been close throughout. Every time Silas would score, Karo would answer, and the lead went back and forth. Leonard had been pleasantly surprised. Even though Alan was still missing, Josh was back and he was playing well. The team had played together and had remained focused throughout the contest. Maybe it was the fact that the two arch rivals were playing each other in what would probably be their very last game ever.

Silas had the lead 31-27 with less than a minute to go. They also had the ball and were driving for another score. It would be a safe strategy to run down the clock and take their slim win with a sigh of relief. But they were greedy. A double digit win would look better. Rivalries sometimes make coaches do strange things. They wanted to run up the score. They were going to pass.

The Silas quarterback brought the team to the line of scrimmage and began the cadence. After three successful pass completions, the Silas coaches had figured on a full blitz by Karo, and they hoped to take advantage of it. They would float their tailback out for a screen pass after a two second delay, and he would follow the pulling linemen around the right side to the end zone. It would be a fitting end to the rivalry, a last minute testament that everyone could remember to mark the end of the history between the two schools.

The Silas coaches had guessed correctly. Jason had called for an all out attack in the defensive huddle. Not only did the Eagles come with the down linemen, but the linebackers were told to rush the passer as well. The cadence was called, and the play began to unfold beautifully for Silas. The Karo secondary was backpedaling with the deep receivers, and everyone else was trying to get to the quarterback.

Everyone except Brad. Something didn't make sense to him. The play showed itself to be a deep pass, but there were no secondary receivers. On every other pass play, Silas had either their tight end cross in the opposite direction, or one of the wide-outs would cut his route short in front of the linebackers. This play had only one single back flaring out of the backfield. Why would they change their passing strategy during the last minute of the game? It suddenly struck him, "because this was not intended to be a deep pass, but to look like one."

Brad's mind quickly raced through the possibilities. What play would benefit the offense the most by getting the other team to fall for the bait of a deep pass? A misdirection? Reverse? NO, A SCREEN PASS! They were setting up a screen, and judging by what he saw developing, they were doing it perfectly. In an instant, he would have to take a gamble. Brad abandoned his receiver and sprinted toward the line of scrimmage. From the corner of his eye, he could see the pulling linemen headed right where he was going. He would have to get around them.

The Silas quarterback saw the play unfolding just like it was supposed to. The pocket was collapsing quicker than he expected because of that

Jason Moeller guy, but the linemen were almost in position. He turned his head and saw his tailback twenty yards away waiting for the ball. Now was the time. Because of Jason, he had to loft the ball higher than he wanted to, but the play was there. They had it in the bank.

But he hadn't figured on Brad. He thought he had everyone fooled. Brad avoided a lineman who dove at his feet. He stumbled, but quickly regained his balance. In front of him, the tailback was stretching his arms upward for the pass. Thank God it had a high arc, because it gave Brad another second to get there. The ball floated down toward the arms of the receiver, but it didn't get there. Brad stepped in front and snatched it right before it got to its destination. It was now an eighty yard foot race to the end zone.

Brad ran as fast as he could, but he knew he would have to go faster. "To accelerate," he thought, "to act or move faster, to hasten the natural or usual course of, to cause to happen ahead of time." He knew he had the advantage of a head start, but it would all depend on the mass and force of the player chasing him. "Force equals mass times velocity, and the force needed to move an object is proportional to its mass times the acceleration. If the force and the initial position and the velocity of a body are given, then subsequent positions and terminal velocity could be computed, although the force may vary with time or position. However, the greater the mass, the slower the change of velocity when a given force is..."

Brad felt an arm on his back. In an instant he was slammed to the ground. He got up slowly and shook his head to clear the cobwebs. "Damn," he thought, "that son of a bitch is fast."

Brad looked up at the scoreboard. Twenty-one seconds remained on the clock. Neither team had ay time-outs. There was time for three plays. First and ten on the twenty-three yard line. He looked to the sideline and saw Coach Davis signaling him to hurry and get the team into a huddle. He would have to take charge.

"I've got three plays," Brad told the team, "and we're going to run them without a huddle. As soon as the first play is over, I want everybody to hustle to the line of scrimmage and set himself for the next play. They are probably going to expect three passes into the end zone, figuring we will go for the touchdown on each play. I am betting they will be in their prevent defense, so we're going to go underneath the coverage for three plays at ten yards a play. The first play will be a ninety tight end cross. We'll come back with a sixty-four flanker curl, and the third play will be a ninety split end corner. The cadence for each play will be the quick count. Questions?" There were none. "Let's make this work," he said. "Ready, break!"

The first play worked perfectly for a ten yard gain out of bounds, and the team hustled to the line of scrimmage forcing Silas to stay with the same defense. The second play was just a good, and after two plays the team found themselves on the seven yard line with six seconds to go. Brad nodded to Josh as he began the cadence. There was single coverage on Josh. If he could sell the inside post route, he might be able to clear himself in the corner. He only had to beat one defender.

The play began with a surprise. Silas brought both backers on a blitz. Brad saw the strategy immediately and sprinted quickly to the pocket. He avoided one tackler and stepped into the protection. He could see Josh making his double move to the outside. It was a move that took a little longer, but it turned the defender completely around, and by the time his opponent finished his circle, Josh was standing alone in the corner of the end zone. The grin on Brad's face was enormous. It was going to work. This game was theirs. He lofted the ball gently into Josh's waiting arms.

Josh dropped the ball. The buzzer sounded. The Silas stands erupted. Silas players began jumping up and down. Brad sank to his knees. Josh stood in the end zone staring at his hands. Jason took off his helmet and walked quietly to the sideline. Leonard walked to the middle of the field and congratulated the Silas coach. He saw William giving Josh a hug. How could he tell his team how proud he was? How could he tell them what a great game they had played? He followed his silent team into the locker room.

"Where the hell did you learn to coach?" he heard from the back of the bleachers.

“How do you think Josh is doing?” Leonard asked. “The poor guy felt miserable Friday after he dropped that pass.”

William nodded in agreement. “I’m sure he heard about it several times from his dad when he got home.” William took another sip of his coffee.

“Or his mom,” Leonard added. “When Linda was alive we would always play a game after one of us had talked to her. Every conversation with her was a litany of criticism, so the one who didn’t have the conversation would have to guess whether her main complaints were about a person, place, or thing. If you guessed right, the other had to load the dishwasher alone that evening.”

William chuckled and took another sip. Samantha sat next to him blowing on her cocoa to cool it down. This Sunday evening was probably the last time the three of them would be able to sit outside and still be comfortable. They were bundled up in their sweaters and jackets and sat together at the picnic table. The chill, humid air made it easy to see their breath when they talked.

“I hear Greg Kent’s mother is going back in the hospital for more tests,” Samantha said. “Have either of you heard anything?” Both of them shook their head “no.”

“But I did hear that Brad goes to Wichita tomorrow to have his interview,” Leonard said. “It will be a long shot for him, because the selective schools have so many applicants, they can find someone to fit any slot they want."

"I got another call from a scout about Jason," William said. "I sent them a film and a glowing letter. His problem is that nobody had really heard about him before, but with the season he's having, I know he will be playing college ball somewhere next year."

"I hope you're right," Leonard said after a sip, "because the last time I talked to him, he said he may not accept any offer to play at any college. He said his mother is not feeling well, and he might stay home to be with her."

Silence descended on the three. They took turns sipping on their steaming cocoa and coffee while visiting their own thoughts. The phone rang in the house, and Samantha got up to answer it. "I'm cold anyway," she said. "I'll get it."

William and Leonard sat silently watching the steam coming off the top of their cups. "It's been a rough week," Leonard finally said.

"A rough week," William echoed.

The back screen door opened and Samantha cast a shadow from the doorway. "William!" she shouted. "You've got a call."

"Who is it?"

"I have no idea. He said his name is Pinky."

In a second, William was out of his chair and sprinting toward the house. Leonard was right behind him.

Sprinkles spotted the windshield as William pulled "old green" into the parking lot in front of the Mid-America All Indian Center. It was the third straight day of rain, but the steady soaking rain of the last two days had given way to a light but steady rain. As he suspected, the parking lot was virtually empty at eight in the morning.

There had been no promises, but Pinky said he had told Alan to "go to the big Indian," Monday morning. "Go to the big Indian," Pinky told him. "I don't remember what the name is, but its downtown where the two rivers meet. It's the big metal Indian where he looks like he's prayin in the wind."

William knew. He had been to the "big metal Indian" many times. He and Samantha often went to the festivals throughout the year. He had been offered a seat on the council, and he was considering it. So it was a familiar sight as he rounded the corner to the back of the building and looked at the "Keeper of the Plains" standing tall and proud fifty feet above the convergence of the Arkansas and Little Arkansas rivers. He strained to see through the drizzle.

He thought he saw a cloaked figure leaning on the rail at the bottom of the statue, peering down. Even from a distance, William could hear the falls where the two rivers met. Usually they flowed silently together at the end of the peninsula, but the rain of the last few days had swollen the rivers so the waters were especially loud. William walked quickly keeping an eye on the figure ahead of him.

The figure heard William come up from behind and turned to see who it was. "Damn, Pinky!" William thought. "I'm going to buy you a whole closet full of clothes." The person who turned around was a big goofy guy about eighteen years old. He was wearing a faded corduroy coat and a beat up leather cowboy hat which was dripping rain from its edges. He flashed a quick, involuntary smile. His name was Alan Burns. William stopped a couple of steps short and the two stood silently looking at each other.

"How are you doing?" William finally asked.

There was shrug of shoulders. "Okay, I guess."

"Where are you staying?"

"I met some people," Alan said. William knew that meant he was probably staying in an abandoned building with some other kids.

William stepped up to the rail and leaned out over the river for a better view. "You know, this would have been a perfect winter camp for my people a couple hundred years ago," he said. "There was plenty of water, good grazing land for the horses, a lot of trees for firewood, and a natural defense on three sides if an enemy were foolish enough to attack." Silent for a moment, he turned to face Alan. "But those times are gone, and they're gone forever."

Alan turned toward William. The rain dripped from the edges of his leather hat in a steady stream. "He must have been waiting out here for a while," William thought.

"I didn't think you'd come," Alan finally said. "I hoped you would, but I didn't know." He turned toward the river again. "I didn't know if anyone even cared."

William braved a hand on the boy's shoulder. It was not rejected. "I want you to come back with me," he said as her turned Alan to face him.

Alan shook his head "no" and his lip started to quiver. "No…I…can never go back there."

"With me," William caught his eye. "I mean, I want you to stay with Samantha and me."

Alan's eyes widened, and he wiped some water from them.

"I promise that neither your mom nor your dad will ever harm you again," William said quietly. "It's time for you to start a new life. Please."

For a moment Alan just stared at the river. He wiped his eyes again, and slowly shook his head "yes." "Okay," he said softly. "I'll do it," he said and wiped his eyes again. "Besides," he said with a forced smile, "I really miss the team, and we've still got three games left."

William laughed aloud as the two figures fell into a hug. The rain fell on them for the longest time before they made their way back to the old pick-up. The "Keeper of the Plains" continued to pray in the wind.

The New Life Academy of Wichita came into existence three years ago as a K-12 school with a total of 60 students. It was inter-denominational Christian school, which meant it was open to all Protestants who thought the public schools were going to hell. The parents who started it had been home-schooling their children to keep them away from the godless influences of an evil society. Their big break came when a rich benefactor died and willed the school a tract of land, and the money to build a new building.

Within two years, the New Life Academy was completed and the enrollment was up to two-hundred. Immediately the school began adding sports. They started with basketball, track and tennis. The following year it was golf and volleyball. This year they added football. The director of athletics for the academy had been quick to pencil Karo into their maiden schedule. If they had a chance to win one game this year, he thought it would be their seventh against the Karo Eagles.

But Karo was no longer a team that hung their head when they talked about where they were from. They were no longer full of apology and self-pity. The Silas loss had stung them, but they were coming together as a team and playing some of the best football they had played all year. In fact, they found themselves in a place they would not have considered possible a year ago. They were dominating the opposition.

Karo led 21-0 at the end of the fist quarter. By half-time, it was apparent the contest was well in control, because when the horn sounded for the intermission, Karo led the New Life Academy 31-0. If it hadn't been for two early fumbles, they probably would have scored twice more. When the second half began, Karo scored on an eighty yard drive to make the score 38-0.

"This is weird," Brad said in the huddle. "We could beat these guys a hundred to nothing."

"I know," Jason agreed. "It's like there's no challenge. It's not even much fun."

"Let's do it," Josh said. "Let's go for a hundred."

There was silence in the huddle. They looked over at the team opposite them. How many years had they been the ones with their heads down, their eyes blank, with no joy of battle, and no self-respect.

"No," Jason said firmly. "Never degrade an opponent," he said to the huddle. "We shouldn't try to embarrass them." The silence continued.

"Nobody can get better if you just give them something," Brad said. "They have to earn it. All we can do is encourage them, and tell them when they've done a good job."

"Let's play hard," Greg said, "but let's not run up the score. Coach would never do that. We shouldn't either." There was unanimous agreement, and they broke the huddle to defend the field.

The next play, the New Life Academy ran a sweep round the right end. They pulled both guards to lead as the quarterback made a reverse pivot and pitched the ball to the tailback. The play was dead before it began. Alan was on an outside slant from his tackle position and flowed right toward the ball. The New Life Academy fullback saw Alan's angle of pursuit, and so he cut his path to intercept Alan. It was a good block, and Alan was knocked completely off his feet. But Jason was already past the line of scrimmage from his linebacker position. He made the tackle for a three yard loss.

Alan got up and applauded the New Life fullback. "Good block," he said as he clapped his hands a couple of times. "Good block," he repeated as he nodded approvingly. The New Life fullback looked confused for an instant and then walked back to his huddle.

The next play was a fullback trap. Greg read the trap immediately from his linebacker position and shot the gap. The playside guard saw him coming and tried a reach block, and he was able to contact Greg with his right shoulder. Greg suddenly found himself falling through the air to the ground with the New Life blocker on top of him. All Greg could do was reach out his hand in an attempt to grab the leg of the ball carrier. He got the ankle. The fullback tripped, staggered, and fell after a gain of a yard.

"Nice job," Greg tapped his opponent on the shoulder. "I was lucky to get him."

"Thanks," came the reply. "You guys are pretty good." There was a brief hesitation. "We suck," he said and his eyes immediately went to the ground.

"Keep at it," Greg said. "You can't feel bad if you try your best."

The opponent walked back to the huddle with his head turned toward Greg and a smile on his face. All over the field, players form both teams were talking with each other like they had known each other for years. There were sharing laughs, congratulations, and acts of sportsmanship without regard to the color of the jersey.

On the ensuing punt return, one of the New Life players sprinted around the wall of blockers and made a great tackle before Jason could gain more than a few yards. It seemed as if there were as many Karo players who congratulated him as there were from his own team.

It was a joy to watch, and Leonard swelled with pride. Both teams were playing hard and enjoying the game. The New Life players had regained their pride, and in fact, traded touchdowns in the fourth quarter. The game ended with a fierce goal-line stand that had the Karo players congratulating their opponents on their effort. The final score was 45-7, but when the game was over, the two teams walked of together as if there had not been a winner or a loser.

Tiffany Edwards turned on the cappuccino machine and pulled biscotti from the cabinet. She took a bite and opened the refrigerator door. "Chris," she called over her shoulder, "are you taking the Beemer or the Caddy today?"

"Beemer," came the shouted answer.

"Did you pack a lunch for me?" The question went into the refrigerator.

"I thought you were going to the club for lunch," came the answer from the bedroom. "Didn't you say you had a golf date with the head of Everson and Boyles?"

Tiffany frowned and closed the door. "I got out of it," she answered. "Judy agreed to take my place so I could finish the Turner project." She sighed and took another bit of her biscotti. Christopher walked into the kitchen straightening his tie. "I guess I'll have to order in," she said with a sigh.

"I've got a good feeling about our meeting tomorrow with management," Chris said as he grabbed a cup and waited for the cappuccino machine to finish. "Those guys will be glad to get a facility that can be up and running in less than a year. We are really behind in production. I read where they were expecting to complete seven units a month, but are so constricted by space they can barely make five. They will think it was a stroke of luck to have found such a property on such sort notice." He paused and rinsed his cup with warm water from the sink faucet. "I think the only question they will ask is "when can we begin production?"

"And how much will they be willing to offer?" Tiffany asked. "That's the most important thing."

Christopher leaned in and kissed her on the cheek. She softly brushed him back. "Don't mess my make-up," she protested. "We'll have plenty of time for fun and games after we close the deal."

"So which makes you hotter?" Chris ventured, "me or money?"

Tiffany tilted her head a moment. "I don't know. You both fulfill different needs. I guess it's a tie," she said with a knowing smile.

Chris gave her a playful spank as she walked away toward the closet to get her coat.

"I don't have time for this," Tiffany said as she put her coat over her arm and headed for the front door. "Don't forget to leave the grocery list for Angelica, and tell her to make sure the salmon is fresh. The last time she bought seafood I almost got sick."

"Yes dear," Chris answered in monotone. How many times had he given the same response? He turned to the cappuccino machine as it finished its work. At times she could be such a bitch. But, he figured, if it got too bad he could drop her and she wouldn't soak him too much. The pre-nup would see to that. She had her money and he had his. Besides, a year from now they both would have a lot more of it.

"Oh my God," Chris heard a kind of wail coming from Tiffany. He turned around to see her frozen in the doorway staring out through the front door. Her mouth was open and her coat was slowly slipping from her hands to the floor. Her eyes were fixed.

Chris took a few steps toward her. "What's wrong?" he asked and quickened his pace. "What's the matter?" He turned his head when he came to the door. He grimaced at what he saw. The two stood motionless and speechless.

Their four wheel drive, all purpose, all terrain, sports utility vehicle was unharmed in every way, but it was sitting sideways in their garage door.

The crisp October night was just cool enough that most fans had to put on their jackets. There were a few guys who associated manliness with discomfort and they sat in the bleachers in their t-shirts and shorts insisting time and again that they really weren't cold. For the players, however, the weather was perfect. Hardly a breath of wind stirred, and the cool weather would keep them from cramping. It was an absolutely gorgeous evening.

The game had been close from the opening kickoff. Defense ruled the night. The fist half had ended in a scoreless tie. During the third quarter, a turnover by both teams led to the only scores. The Karo Eagles were down 8-7 and the final quarter was more than half over.

Leonard couldn't figure out how the Walton High School defense worked. No matter the alignment, no matter the option called, the Walton defenders were waiting for the ball carrier. Was there a key they were following that made every play predictable? It seemed like the Walton linebackers made the correct guess on every play. Luck like that would win you a million dollars in Vegas.

Maybe they weren't guessing. Maybe somehow, they knew. Was it possible that they had figured out what every play was going to be? But how would they do that? The alignment only varied with the distance of the wide receivers. Walton couldn't know what the play was going to be because Karo didn't know what the play was going to be until Brad called the audible from the line.

That was it! Of course! Somehow Walton had figured out the audible system! They knew the live colors, the blocking calls, and which back would carry the ball by listening to Brad! No wonder their defense was doing so well. Before every play, Brad was telling them exactly what to do.

"Time out!" Leonard shouted to the nearest official. "Time out!" The umpire granted the request and Leonard called the team over. "They've figured us out," Leonard said as they gathered around him, "and we've got less than a minute to invent a new audible system," he said. "I don't know how they did it, but they figured out our calls, and they know exactly what each play is going to be. Any suggestions.?"

"No more audibles," Alan said. "We call every play in the huddle, and only give dummy calls." He took a long drink from the water bottle.

"Let's keep the audibles," Brad said as he took the water bottle from Alan, "and give them misinformation." Brad took a drink himself and continued. "We call a play in the huddle, and then we go to the line and give them the live color, blocking calls, and option reads just like we always do." He took another drink. "Only we don't run the play we give them. We run the play from the huddle."

"Even better," Jason said. "Let's give them an audible that will lead them in the opposite direction of where we're really going." Jason turned to face Brad. "Can you take our play and turn it around for them?"

"Sure," Brad shook his head. "I'll transpose the play in my head and give that to them." There were nods of agreement.

"Great" Leonard said. "We've got to get one more score. I'd hate to lose this game by one point."

The Umpire blew his whistle and quickly called both teams back on the field. Brad called them all together in the huddle. "Okay," he said as he strapped his helmet back on, "the play is going to be an 18 White Keeper. Any audible you hear will be intended to mislead those guys on the other side of the ball, so pay no attention to it. When you hear the audible call, I want you to make your blocking calls exactly like you would if we were running that play. Got it? 18 White Keeper, delay count. Ready? Break." The team broke the huddle together and ran to the line of scrimmage.

It was the quickest scoring drive of the season. In two plays, Karo completely fooled the defense and gained thirty yards. Walton did exactly as predicted. They flew to the audible call without regard for any other play. The ploy fooled them completely, and the Eagles scored on the third play to pull ahead by five. The two point conversion failed, and the score stood at 13-8. If Karo's defense could hold for the last three minutes, they would have their fourth win of the year.

The rest of the fourth quarter remained a defensive battle as Brad discovered that feeding the opponent false information no longer worked. Walton paid no attention to the audible calls anymore. The ruse had worked for the first series, but that was it. They weren't going to fool Walton anymore during this game. But they were ahead by five. If they could just hold on.

The last minute seemed to go on forever as Leonard looked up nervously several times at the clock. Walton had the ball on their own 37 yard line. They threw another pass. If fell incomplete. Walton had two more plays to make the gain. Leonard looked at the clock again. Less than half a minute to go. Surely his team could defend 63 yards of field for twenty-three seconds. Leonard was confident they could ride this one out. Just a couple more plays and it would be over.

Walton ran a reverse to their flanker. Jason missed the tackle. Brad was blocked to the ground. Alan tripped over him, and Greg took a poor pursuit angle. Leonard's heart sank. He watched as if it were a bad dream. The Walton back was sprinting up the sideline in the clear. He had nobody between him and the goal line.

Leonard crossed his arms over his chest. The Walton back had good speed and a clear path. Only Josh had a chance to catch him, and he was ten yards behind. Leonard watched as the ball carrier ran up the sideline. He shook his head in frustration. They would lose another game in the last seconds.

But Josh was giving great pursuit. It almost looked like he was gaining on the ball. Leonard found himself shaking his head in disbelief. Josh was not quitting in his pursuit, he was closing the distance. What made Josh think he could catch that guy? Josh couldn't beat half of his own team in a sprint. Could he get him in time?

Josh was doing exactly that. He was gaining on him. It was the most extraordinary effort Leonard had seen from any member of his team all year long. He pumped his fist in the air trying to make Josh run faster. He saw Josh leap at the last second and make the tackle. The ball carrier came to the ground on the three yard line. The game was not over. Karo was still alive.

Walton used a time-out now and they still had one left. There were eleven seconds left to play in the game. Walton would have time for one play, maybe two. Leonard turned to William. "Well, coach," he said as he took his hat off and rubbed his forehead. "Any ideas?"

"Key the fullback," William answered quickly. "They're going to lead with him as a blocker on an isolation play. We have to get Jason to mirror him form the middle linebacker and have him shoot the gap that the fullback leads him to." Leonard nodded in agreement and motioned to William. "Go give them the plan." William sprinted out to the player's huddle in the end zone. "Take some water out to the field!" Leonard shouted to the trainers.

Leonard looked for a water bottle himself. His mouth was dry. He could feel his heart pounding. Was he afraid, or was he just having a wonderful time? Was he excited and happy, or was he scared to death? Why should he care so much? After all, it was just a game.

The time out was over. William came sprinting back to the sidelines as fast as his battered old knees would take him. "All set," he said, and they both turned to watch. The chains were set. First and goal on the three. In eleven seconds they would either win or lose a two hour contest.

Walton called the cadence. The quarterback whirled around and faked a hand-off to the fullback. It was an isolation play just as William had predicted. In a flash, Jason slanted behind the fullback and met the ball carrier in a massive collision. For a moment, neither could gain an advantage, but the Karo pursuit quickly caught up with Jason and the ball carrier was turned back. Walton had gained well over two and a half yards. Barely six inches lay between the ball and the end zone.

"Time out!" the Walton quarterback shouted and motioned to the referee. "Time out! Time out!" The official quickly waved his arms above his head and granted the request. The home-cooking of the timekeeper made sure the game was not over. Two seconds remained on the clock. There was time for one more play.

When Leonard turned to William this time, he saw him already running out on the field toward the Karo huddle. Leonard found another water bottle and took another drink. He was not thirsty, but he had to do something. He wondered what his blood pressure was at this moment.

Leonard saw William jogging back to the sideline. He was back too quickly. What was he doing? The time out was not over. Jason was with him, and he was holding his helmet. This was not good. An official was escorting the two of them to the sideline. "Coach," he shouted, "number 33 has to replace that broken chinstrap on his helmet before he can participate."

Leonard's heart fell. He watched as William and Jason rushed toward the bench. There was a mad scramble at the trainer's kit. Leonard looked at William. "We don't have any time-outs, do we?" William shook his head no, and began digging in the equipment box for some tools.

"Coach!" the official called. "Get a player out here."

Leonard looked around him. Nobody could do half the job Jason did on the goal line. Whoever he sent in would almost certainly not be able to stop the Walton tailback. He looked over at the trainer's table and saw William and Jason feverishly prying on some part of the helmet with a screwdriver.

"Hurry up, coach," Leonard turned back to see the official call again for another player. "The time out is over. Get somebody out here," he ordered.

"Coach," Leonard felt a familiar tug on his sleeve. "Coach, choose me to play." Leonard looked down in disbelief. Ilir was tugging at Leonard's sleeve. "I know the American football," he insisted, "and I know many rules."

Leonard cut him off. "Ilir," he said calmly, "how many games have you played in so far this year?"

"I do not play for any games," Ilir answered, "but I can play the American football and I know many rules."

Leonard shrugged inside. What did it matter? Ilir wouldn't make a difference anyway. Ilir would finally get in a game, and his chances of getting hurt in one play were small.

"Go out there and tell Greg to go to the middle linebacker for Jason," Leonard ordered, "and you take his place at the end."

"Yes, coach," Ilir shouted grinning from ear to ear. "I go play the American football." With that, he turned and sprinted out to the huddle with the rest of the team.

Leonard suddenly realized he was standing with his mouth wide open. What in the world had he just done? He had sent a ninety pound Albanian into the biggest play of the game. He turned his head hoping he would see his star player ready to go back in, but the helmet was not cooperating.

The Karo huddle greeted Ilir with a measure of disbelief and resignation. What the hell was he doing out here? But their frustration didn't last. Like their coach, they knew that without Jason, they didn't really have a chance to stop Walton. They accepted Ilir into the huddle and called the defensive play.

The official gave the ready-for-play signal, blew his whistle and backed away from the ball. The Walton quarterback went under center. "Down!" he shouted in anticipation of the snap. But it didn't come. Ilir stepped across the line of scrimmage and tapped the Walton end on the shoulder pad.

A whistle immediately blew. It was a dead ball foul so there would be no play. As a penalty, the ball would be marked half the distance to the goal line. The crowd in the stands moaned. Half the team threw up their hands. Second and six inches had now become second and three inches.

Leonard looked over at William. He was still working on the helmet. Walton re-huddled and came up to the line. The ready for play whistle blew, and Leonard turned his attention to the game. Again the players were set, and again the quarterback went under center and began his cadence. Again Ilir stepped across the line and tapped the Walton end on the shoulder. A whistle sounded. There would be no play. A three inch gap now became an inch and a half.

Brad walked up to Ilir and grabbed a hold on top of Ilir's helmet. "What are you doing?" his question was more of a shout. "Every time you jump over the line you get a penalty and they get half the distance to the goal!"

Ilir's helmet did not move as he shook his head in agreement. "Yes," he said, "but they do not score."

Brad released his grip on Ilir's helmet. The confused look on his face prompted Ilir to explain. "The penalty to do this is always half the way, but the rules can never award a touchdown."

Brad shook his head. Ilir was right. "You're doing this on purpose?" he asked.

"Yes," Ilir said. "They do not score," he shrugged his shoulders, "and Jason will soon return."

The ready for play whistle blew again. Brad pointed a finger at Ilir as if to say something, but whirled around and went back to his safety position. The Walton quarterback set himself under center and made the first call, but before he finished, Ilir stepped across the line and tapped the end on the shoulder. There was another loud, collective moan from the stands as the whistle blew. Second and an inch and a half would now become second and three quarters of an inch.

Leonard looked out at the field of play and threw up his hands in disbelief. Why would Ilir make the same mistake three times in a row? He wasn't that stupid. "Well," he thought to himself, "I have more responsibility for what is going on out on the field than anybody else. I probably shouldn't have let him go out there in the first place."

The referee walked calmly to Ilir and was greeted by a toothy grin. "Son," he said in his best grandfather voice, "are you slow?"

"I play the American football," Ilir said through his grin.

"He's from Albania," Brad broke in. "He's just not very sure what's going on." The referee looked again at Ilir and grunted.

"I play the American football," Ilir said with an even wider smile.

The referee shook his head and walked away. He blew his whistle declaring the ball ready for play.

"We got it!" William shouted as he and Jason sprinted from the bench to join Leonard at the sideline. The buckle snap was bent, and we had to pry it off with pliers, but we got it." Jason took a few steps onto the field before Leonard pulled him back. "It's too late," Leonard said. "The ball is ready for play."

The Walton quarterback went under center. Once again Ilir stepped across the line to tap the opposing end on the shoulder. This time, however, the Walton end shot out to greet him. In a flash, Ilir was on his back. His helmet was sideways, and his nose was bleeding. Brad ran up to confront the Walton player, but the referee was already backing him away. Before anything else could develop, the official sent both players to their respective huddles.

Ilir was on his feet now. His legs were wobbling, and his nose was a dark purple. Several of his teammates helped him make his way to the sideline until the trainers were able to get him off the field. He looked up and saw Jason sprinting into the game. "I think," Ilir said as if in a dream, "I play enough American football."

"George!" the linesman called to the referee. "What's half of three quarters?" The referee scratched his head.

Jason ran into the huddle and called everyone together.

"Five eighths," Brad called to the head linesman. "Half of three-quarters of an inch is five eighths of an inch," He turned back into the huddle.

"One play!" Jason exclaimed to the team. "We can do this! Alan, I want you and Derek to pinch the "A" gaps, and Josh will mirror the fullback. Greg and Jeremy will slant into the "B" gaps and Brad will shadow the quarterback. I will key on the tailback. This time I think they're going to fake to the fullback and hand off in the other direction. We can make this work. One play. All we have to do is win this one play. We can do it. We focus. We concentrate. We believe."

The whistle blew for the ball to be put in play, and the Karo Eagles ran to get in position. Every muscle, every nerve, every breath was focused on this one play. The Walton quarterback called the cadence.

The ball was snapped, and the Walton quarterback whirled around to fake a hand off to the fullback. So far, Jason had been right. The tailback was taking his counter step and headed full speed toward the opposite side of the fullback. The line of scrimmage suddenly became a wall of bodies colliding with each other. Jason read the counter play and sprinted toward the ball carrier. He could see the Walton player coiling to jump over the pile of players, so Jason jumped into the air as well. The line of scrimmage was a tangle of bodies and sounds. It was like a living, breathing creature wrestling with itself.

Jason and the ball carrier collided in mid-air and struggled above the fray on the ground. They paid no attention to the battle that raged under them. To them it seemed like minutes, but it was over in a split second. The horn blew signaling the end of the game. The pair dropped to the ground a foot from the end zone. Jason had stopped him. The game was over. Karo had held. They had won their fourth game of the year.

Leonard didn't remember much about the next hour. He had been so busy receiving congratulations from everyone. He remembered congratulating Walton on a great game. He knew he had talked with their coach for a while. He remembered lots of celebrating in the locker room, and he remembered a hug from William. He remembered he had left behind all thoughts of Elaine for a while.

About half-way into the hour and a half bus ride home, the celebration still had not lessened. In fact, the team was singing. It was a strange choice, Leonard thought. An old Neal Sedaka tune. Where did that come from? But they were all singing, led by Greg, Brad and Ilir. Ilir was leading the chorus and he did not miss a word. Leonard could only smile. The bus was filled with pure, youthful joy. It was an uninhibited expression of happiness. Leonard suddenly felt sorry for anyone who had not experienced such complete jubilation. He even joined the team in a chorus or two.

"Come-ah, come-ah, down dooby do down down!"

"Come-ah, come-ah, down dooby do down down!

"Don't take your love......away from me..."

"Don't you leave my heart in misery...."

The voices rang with pure joy. The harmony was terrible, but the time flew by.

William pushed the gas pedal to the floor. He glanced at his watch and clenched his jaw. He was ten minutes behind schedule. Monica Lewis had made them wait again while her mom stood in the front doorway and waved at William to hold the bus. William watched her alternately shout something inside the house and then turn to him and call that "she would be right out." Of course she wasn't. She finally did appear in the doorway with her coat, lunch and books cradled in her arms. She said something to her mom and got an earful back in return. William sighed. It seemed like every day it was the same thing with these two.

He glanced at his watch again. If there were no trains crossing on K-68, he still might be able to make up some time. Niclolas and Russell were next, and if they were ready, that would help a lot as well. But if there were any more delays anywhere on the route, he would never get to school on time. The bus rumbled over the gravel road, kicking up a cloud of dust as it went up the hill.

William pulled the bus over the crest of the hill and slowed to look for the two boys at the end of the drive. He couldn't find them. Another delay. They must still be at the house, he told himself, and he would have to drive an extra quarter mile to pick them up. Then some movement on the other side of the road caught his eye. He did a double take. Something wasn't right. Nicholas and Russell were climbing a tree down the road about a hundred feet from their stop.

In an instant, William knew what was happening. He had feared it all year, and prayed that it wouldn't happen, but there it was. A cold chill went through his body. He slowed the bus to get a better look. One of the boys, no both boys, had climbed a scrubby Mulberry tree along the fence line. William could see the older boy, Nicholas, was up about eight feet in the tree. The younger boy, Russell, was hanging from a low lying branch. Out of the tall grass, three dark forms were jumping and snapping at the lowest boy. Occasionally, one of the dogs would latch onto the hanging figure's backpack, furiously twisting and pulling at it.

Nicholas was reaching down and pulling with all his strength to help Russell up into one of the safe branches. Tears were streaming down his face. He was losing the battle. Russell had his legs over a branch and struggled to pull himself up. The two boys were barely able to maintain the status quo as Russell's backpack was being shredded. The three animals below howled their excitement as millennia of instincts told them they were about to have a kill.

William slid the bus to a stop and turned off the engine. He knew in an instant that Russell would lose the struggle, and would not be able to make it safely into the higher branches. The dogs were too big, too strong. In short time Russell would be pulled down. Nicholas clung desperately to him. A shoulder strap slipped off Russell's backpack and dangled halfway to the ground. Instantly a pair of powerful jaws clamped on it shaking it and tearing at it in a frenzy.

William wiped his mouth with his sleeve. The bus was completely silent. The chatter and laughter that had filled the bus seconds before had been replaced by horrible silence. Only the occasional gasp or whimper could be heard. William stood up and reached behind the driver's seat to grab the push broom. He unscrewed the broom head from the handle and turned to everyone in the seats. "Monica," he said sternly. "Get on the radio and call the bus barn. Tell them we have an emergency and to get someone out here now."

William dropped the broom head to the floor, and looked at the passengers intensly. "No matter what happens," he said, "everyone will stay on this bus until help arrives." He knew he would be obeyed. He stepped out of the bus and closed the door behind him.

William broke the broom handle over his knee and suddenly he had a sharp wooden stake in each hand. He looked up just in time to see Russell being pulled from the branch to the ground. First one leg, then the other slipped off the branch. Nicholas strained one last time to keep his little brother from danger, but he was no match. A pair of powerful jaws clamped on a foot, pulling their prey to the ground. Instantly the three dogs were on him. Nicholas screamed from the branch above. The bus erupted with different screams.

William charged toward the dogs. He was screaming as well. It was a primal, savage scream. It was a challenge, a call to blood, a call to battle. It told the world, "it is a good day to die."

One of the dogs saw William approaching and turned to accept the challenge. The beast broke from the prey on the ground and ran to meet William. They would have met head on at full speed, but as the dog instinctively leaped toward William's throat, William instantly dropped to a knee and brought his left arm in a stabbing motion upward into the attacker. The broken end of the broom handle made a crunching sound as it penetrated the ribs of the savage beast, and the dog came down on Williams's side, snapping and snarling.

William felt part of his left shoulder suddenly erupt in pain. He heard the sound of tearing cloth. But just as suddenly as the dog had clenched onto him, he let go and began an immediate retreat, snapping at the broom handle sticking out of his side. William watched as the dog immediately collapsed to the ground on the blowing grass pulling at the object of his pain. The brown grass quickly became red.

William should not have watched his retreating foe. That instant he wasted with his head turned was an instant he was not preparing. He heard something and whirled around, but before he could get off his knee, the other two were on him. The other half of the broom handle went flying from his hand. He tried to gain his feet, but it was impossible. They were both on him. He heard the curious sound of cracking bone. He felt something warm flow over his right ear. He felt flesh being pulled away from his leg. He was surrounded by the growls of the happy beasts, excited and fully animal.

He could not get up, the dogs were too strong. It was all he could do to protect his throat. Out of the corner of his eye he saw where the broom handle had fallen and he began to roll toward it. What seemed like minutes was a matter of seconds until he was there. He felt new stabs of pain and warm sensations of his own blood flowing over different parts of his body. He wanted to curl into a ball and cry out in agony. They were tearing him apart.

William finally rolled over the broom handle and flailed it wildly around him. The tip of the stake grazed the head of one of the dogs as it snapped at his arm and missed. But William saw his chance. He glanced quickly where the animal was going to attack next and plunged into the beast's left shoulder. He heard an instantaneous yelp as the broom handle sank deeply into the dog. The wounded animal immediately withdrew in a fury of anger, confusion, and pain biting at the stake protruding from him.

William did not waste any time looking at the wounded animal. He turned around immediately to find the remaining dog. He didn't know how long he could hold on. He couldn't count the number of places on his body that were throbbing in pain. Perhaps the other dog had been scared away. He prayed the good Great Spirit would make it so. He struggled to a knee.

William heard a growl behind him, and without a weapon and still on a knee, he turned toward the sound. The dog leaped and was suddenly on William. William found himself flat on his back with the dog struggling to get to his throat. It bared its teeth as it came down toward the jugular. William threw his hands out to meet the dog and grabbed it by the throat. It took every ounce of strength he had to keep the dog from ripping open his neck.

For a moment, William wasn't sure he could hold him off. The fierce animal's teeth scraped his skin and drew blood. They were literally nose to nose. The dog growled in anger and anticipation. He was so close to the lethal bite, yet he could not get there. William looked into the eyes of the beast. They were filled with fire and fury. They were ready for the kill. William met the stare with the eyes of cold steel. He too, was ready for the kill.

William began to squeeze his hands around the throat of the attacker.

At first, the dog paid little attention. But gradually, William could feel his grip beginning to crush the windpipe of the animal. In an instant, the dog changed its mind, and what had been a full force for attack, suddenly became a pull of retreat. But William would have none of it. He held his foe firmly, all the time squeezing the very breath out of the beast.

The dog began to flail around but could not break William's vice-like grip. The dog's primal growls became snaps of anger and fear. He could not escape. He alternately lunged and retreated to get away, but he could not. William continued to hold his grip until the beast lay motionless on top of him. William dropped the dog to his side.

The world was spinning. William made it to his knees, lost his balance and fell. He felt a hand on his shoulder. Nicholas had come down from the tree to help. Behind him was Russell, standing with a few scratches and bruises, but standing nonetheless. William struggled to sit up, and collapsed again.

"I'm sorry, Mr. Roundtree," Russell said through tears.

"I know," William said, and then everything went black.

The hospital room was dimly lit and eerily quiet. Leonard sat alone on the edge of his chair leaning in toward William. Samantha had gone out of the room to catch a bite to eat in the cafeteria. She had been with William non-stop, but she had to eat something. She was told that William had a good chance of survival, but if he did, he would very likely have a long recovery.

Leonard flashed back to Linda. How many times had he sat in a chair like this during her final days? With his eyes, he followed the I.V. from the plastic bag to where it was taped to William's forearm. There was a steady drip of clear liquid from the bag. On the other side of the bed, another I.V. went into the other arm. It contained a yellow liquid.

William was sleeping, no doubt a result of the pain-killers he was given. His face was covered with bandages. Underneath the gauze, Leonard could see where William's scalp had been shaved. He could see stitches and sutures. Around the right eye, the swelling and discoloration were the most apparent. The doctor wasn't sure if William would be able to see out of that eye anymore.

There were bandages all over William's body. Yellow-red liquid oozed constantly from each. Much of the muscle of his right shoulder and left calf had to be re-attached. But William's breathing was steady and deep. Monitor after monitor measured every breath and heartbeat with an orchestra of beeps, but Leonard didn't hear them.

"How could anyone have such a big heart?" Leonard thought as he looked upward. "Great Spirit," Leonard suddenly said in a whisper, "this is my friend, William Roundtree. He is a warrior and a sage. I thank you that I have been able to know him for all these years. I thank you for allowing me to laugh and to cry with him. I thank you for the cold that made us shiver, and the heat that made us sweat. I thank you for our triumphs, and our losses. I thank you for the times of hunger and thirst, and our times of plenty. You have been most kind to us. But today, if you send death down to meet him, he will do you battle, for he is not ready to leave this world. Please," Leonard finished his prayer, "let him live another day."

Leonard lowered his head, and wiped a tear from his eye. "I never had a brother," he said to the sleeping figure, "until I met you. You don't know how much you helped me after Linda died. I can never repay your friendship." Leonard paused and sighed heavily. "I'm afraid," he said. "I lost Linda, I'm losing Elaine, and now I may lose you."

The beeping of the machines and the labored breathing were the only response. For another hour Leonard just watched William sleep. He didn't notice when Samantha came back into the room. It was well into the evening when he left the hospital to go home.

He made his way down the hall to the side entrance. He could see a heavy drizzle falling outside and passing cars were spraying a thin film of water over everything they passed. Leonard stopped under the overhanging door to fill and light his pipe out of the weather. He offered his lighter to a nurse who had come out on her break to have a smoke. She thanked him, and they stood quietly outside as Leonard decided whether to make a run for the car, or wait out the rain.

A middle-aged woman wearing a fake fur coat and carrying a large black umbrella stepped outside the door. In spite of the rain, she decided to walk to her car. "You smokers are pathetic," she said as she opened her umbrella and walked off.

Brad pulled the mail from the mailbox and scanned the return addresses of all the letters. There is was. He had finally heard from the admissions board. This was what he'd been working for his whole life. Finally he would know. He put his thumb under a corner and ripped open the envelope tearing half the top away as he did. He was so nervous, he accidentally held the letter upside down for a moment, and then turned it and began to read.

"Dear Brad,

'Thank you for your application. As you are aware there are approximately eight thousand applications each year for two thousand spots in the freshmen class." Brad didn't have to read more than a few seconds. He lowered the paper to his side and closed his eyes. He didn't make it. All the work, all the stress, all the energy he had devoted had been fruitless. His application had been flawless, and he thought, the interview had gone really well. What had he done wrong? What the hell could he have done differently? Was his dad not rich or famous enough? Did he not have a good enough last name?

Brad raised the letter again and re-read the first paragraph. He wadded the paper up in his hands. Funny how a little thing like a letter could determine a destiny. A few lines, a few words formed a different way, and he would have been jumping up and down, screaming with joy. His plans would have been set in motion, his future would have been determined.

Now nothing seemed certain. He had tried to run out in front with the big dogs and was told he couldn't. He wasn't good enough. He would have to go back and join the rest of the pack. He would have to join the average and be happy with his mediocrity. He could do that. He could work at half-speed and stay in the middle. He could secretly despise those who surrounded him.

Maybe he was fooling himself. Maybe he belonged with the mediocre. Maybe he should embrace his mediocrity. After all, he was just a hick from Karo. Did he think he could ever rise above that? In fact, he could be the king of the mediocre. He could even start his own church and gain tax-free status. The First Church of the Mediocre!

He would be their leader, Reverend Brad. He would have a multitude of parishioners whose life goal was to never think, act, or feel anything beyond the average. Thousands of the mediocre would flock to his sermons and hear about the dangers of looking beyond the mean, median and mode. The First Church of the Mediocre would make him rich by buying his books, videos and disks warning about the dangers of excellence. That was it. That was his true calling. He would lead the lemmings. He would be in charge of failure. He was eminently qualified.

He would not change the world. He would put his dreams on a shelf and let them collect dust like some old bowling trophy. On an odd occasion, he would pull them down, blow off the dust and shake his head at how foolish he had been. The world doesn't care, why should he? The world didn't need nor welcome dreamers. He was king of the mediocre and that was good enough. He might as well accept it and get on with his mundane life.

Brad threw the letter on the ground at the base of the mailbox. He had just contributed litter to the problems of the world and he didn't care. "That's what mediocre people do," he thought. "Good or bad, right or wrong, they just don't give a damn."

Brad turned and walked into the house. The letter rolled down the street with the south wind.

Jason ran up the front porch steps into the house waving the letter in his hand. His dad's car was not yet in the drive. "Guess what!" he shouted as he raced inside. "I got the scholarship! I got a letter asking me to play football next year! Mom! Mom!"

There was no answer. His mom must be in bed again. Jason wondered if he should go to coach Davis's house and show him the letter, or continue into his mother's bedroom and tell her.

"Jason?" came a weak call from behind the door. "Jason is that you?"

Jason opened the door and quickly went to his mother's bedside. "Look at this letter I just got in the mail," he said excitedly. He sat on the edge of the bed and tried to control his enthusiasm. "It says I've got a full scholarship to play college football next year."

His mother did not read the letter, but scanned the letterhead. She began to shake her head. "Oh, no, oh, my," she repeated softly. "That school is a hundred miles away from here. That won't do...I'm not strong enough yet...your father is too busy...I need you to stay home and help."

"MOM!" Jason shouted and leapt to his feet. "I have a chance to go to college on a scholarship. I have a chance to keep playing the game I love," he continued to shout. "If I don't take this opportunity, it may never come again. Never!"

"Please don't raise your voice," came the timid reply. "I'm only asking for one year. Is that too much to do for your mother?"

Jason turned around. He didn't want his mother to see how angry he was. He bit his lip to stop it from quivering.

"I'm not well," he heard behind him. "If you could just stay home next year until I get my strength back."

Jason walked to the door without saying a word. He began squeezing the doorknob as hard as he could. Through the door he heard the jingle of keys on the lamp table and the familiar sound of the leather on the recliner accepting its occupant. The television began emitting a jingle about toothpaste. Dad was home.

"Please don't be angry with me," Jason heard a meek voice behind him. "I've had a hard life. My parents died when I was a young girl. It's just until I get my strength back. You can live at home and go to the local junior college for the first year or two. I can't bear to think of you so far away. I hope you love me enough to do that."

Jason let go of the doorknob and wiped a tear from each eye. He did not turn around. "I just thought....this time....you would be happy for me," he said as he wiped each eye again. The laughter from the television's soundtrack came clearly through the door.

"It's just that...I'm not feeling well," the voice behind Jason was begging. "I don't ask for much," it said. "Just one year."

Jason opened the door and headed down the hall toward the front door. None of his senses were working. He was numb. The sounds of a mindless sitcom were unrecognizable.

"I'm going to Brad's," he announced without emotion. "I'll eat there."

His dad grunted acknowledgement and twisted the cap off his first beer. "Don't forget to feed the dog," his dad said as Jason stepped outside.

Greg watched the station wagon pull out of the drive. His mom was resting in the back seat. She waved weakly to everyone saying goodbye on the front lawn. More tests. There were always more tests. One test led to another test which led to another test. They would not end until she was dead.

Greg knew it would soon be over. He knew it because his mother was at peace. If she were still fighting, he would see it, he would sense it. But she was no longer fighting her fate. She was going through the motions. She might choose to hold on until Christmas so she could spend one last holiday season with her family, but that would be it. It was over. She had lost the fight and she was at peace with it.

Greg was not. He turned from the picture window and headed toward the stairs. He had some studying to do. He glanced at the family Bible propped up on the buffet in the living room. He walked over and picked it up. What good had this brought his mom? How did her pious life benefit her now? How much protection did she get from her morning hour of prayer?

He had been taught all his life that God was good. But what kind of "good" God would allow one of his devout servants to suffer and die so needlessly? Why did God always get the glory when things went well, but never the blame when things went bad? His mother could be at peace with those questions, but he could not.

Greg opened and closed the Bible without expression and dropped it in the trash as he went up the stairs.

Even in the dim light Josh could feel the curtains occasionally brush against him. The breeze tonight was strong. He sat in front of his bedroom window looking out at the top of the tree he had helped plant when he was five years old. It was over thirty feet tall now, and he remembered how excited he had been when he helped plant it. He was going to be Tarzan, and this was going to be one of his Tarzan trees. He would build a tree house in it and swing from limb to limb. He would fight jungle animals and save beautiful women in peril.

He had helped plant the orchard in the back yard. Where his parents wanted peaches, pears, and apples, he wanted to be Tarzan, king of the jungle. But as usually happens in real life, things just didn't work out. Either he grew up too fast, or the trees grew too slowly, and he gave up his Tarzan dream. Maybe in another ten years or so, the trees would be large enough for some other five year old to fulfill that fantasy. Things rarely work out as hoped. His time was over. His life had not gone as he planned. Nothing he ever did was right. Nothing he ever did was good enough. He wasn't good enough. He just couldn't cut it. He was a failure.

He couldn't go on disappointing everybody. He had tried and tried and tried, but now he was tired of trying. He just didn't have what it takes. How many times had his mother and father told him that? What was wrong with him? What was it that made him such a loser? He was tired of always coming up short. It didn't matter anymore. It was too late. He would be better off not trying. Everyone would be better off if he would just get out of the way.

He picked up the letter lying on his dresser and read it by the rising moonlight. He wanted to make sure every word was right. He didn't want to screw up the last thing he ever did. It would be just like him to mess that up too. He knew every word by heart, but he read them anyway.

"Dear Mom and Dad,

I would like to tell you how I feel, but feelings are over-rated. Besides, sharing isn't convenient for me. I'm selfish. Crying makes me uncomfortable and love hurts. Always. I trust nothing and no one. Life has very little to offer. You may frown, but we pessimists deal with tragedy well. We have learned not to care, not to expect, not to believe anything so we can never be disappointed.

Happiness, in general, escapes me. Things associated with good cheer, such as bright bold colors, rainbows, church, stupid loud energy…screw all that. It is annoying. It is ugly. I want soft, warm, dark, quiet apathy. I want anarchy. I want sincerity. I want rest. I want an open casket.

I'm sorry I have caused you so much pain. I realize now that I have not been the son you wanted, and I have been a big disappointment. There's nothing I can do to change that. I wish I could. I now know you and everyone else would be better off without me. Please believe me when I say that I tried the best I could. Now you will be able to have a better life. Please forgive me one last time. Love, Josh."

Josh put down the letter and looked out again at the Tarzan tree. Why was life so hard? Why had he been so bad at it? A tear formed on his cheek. He wiped it away. Now was not the time to go soft. He had to be tough. He had to be a man. He had to do the right thing. For once in his life he would do the right thing. There would be no tears. He had the courage to do it, and he was going to get it over with.

He placed the letter on the top of his dresser and slowly opened the top drawer. Under the confusion of underwear and socks, he found the 38 caliber handgun right where he had hidden it. He would use his dad's gun, and the arm that held it would display his brother's initials for all to see.

He had seen it in movies dozens of times. Just put the barrel in your mouth and squeeze with your thumb. The guys in the movies always died instantly. He wouldn't feel a thing. There would be a mess out the back of his head, but that was why the window was open. Sitting with his back to the open window, he wouldn't even splatter the wall. There wouldn't be much to clean up. Maybe his parents would thank him for his consideration. Maybe he would finally get a compliment.

Josh picked up the hand gun and rolled it around in his hands. He had held it many times before. It felt strangely heavy this time. He looked out at the Tarzan tree one more time. It had lost almost all its leaves now. Those that still clung to life were dark shadows against the moon. His last thoughts would be of him swinging on the Tarzan tree, giving the Tarzan yell, and being five years old.

He turned around so the back of his head was against the open window, and set the gun on his lap. He glanced at the clock radio. The digital display read 11:58. It was almost time. At midnight he would end the pain. He would never disappoint anyone ever again. He closed his eyes. No last thoughts. No great debate was taking place. His mind was clear. He didn't care enough to stop. He only regretted not playing his last game.

Josh sat with his eyes closed. He felt neither time nor motion. He felt nothing. There were, however, sounds. Was it music or was it the wind? Soft whispering? Was it a chorus of voices? Flashes of twisted sounds were instantly growing and fading all around him. They seemed to be backed by an unholy chorus. They were chanting to him, for him. "You can do it," they said in a strange tongue. "You can join us."

Josh tightened his closed eyes as if to drive them away. Instantly there were hundreds more of those voices blending together, wailing and whispering the same thing to him. "Join us." "You can do it." Josh raised the gun to his mouth and opened wide. The barrel of the gun tasted acrid on his tongue. The voices grew louder in a crescendo of glee and joy. "You can do it!" they wailed. "You can join us!" He was entranced by the sound. It held him spellbound. It was time to follow the voices. It was time to join in the chorus. It was time to end the pain.

But something in the music didn't fit. There was another sound that didn't belong with the moaning and wailing from this chorus of another world. What else was he hearing? Was it laughter? Not an evil, sadistic laugh, but real human laughter? Someone was full of joy. Someone was so happy he couldn't contain it. Josh could feel tears streaming down his face. It was like he used to laugh when he was a kid playing in the Tarzan tree. Was this his last taunt? Would he die hearing a chorus from hell backed up by a laugh of joy?'

The chorus quickly grew louder as it sensed the completion of the task at hand. It tried to silence everything else, and for an instant, the laughter was gone. Josh began to squeeze the trigger. But the laughter came back. It didn't fit. It was not part of the unholy choir. It was not part of the other world, it was part of this world. It was coming from his window. There was someone laughing outside his window.

Now the chorus raged and cursed at Josh. The voices growing and fading before him were no longer beckoning, but ordering. "Do it!," they commanded. "Join us!" But there it was again. He heard a laugh. Josh opened his eyes.

Instantly the choir and the voices disappeared in a howl of protest. Josh looked down at the gun and slowly removed it from his mouth. "What am I doing?" he thought.

There it was again. There were several laughs this time. There was someone or some group laughing outside his window. He dropped the gun to his lap and turned in his chair to look outside. In the pale light he could see a group gathered under the Tarzan tree. They were carrying something large. Now and then one of them would try to stifle a laugh and the others would shush him while trying not to laugh themselves. They were admonishing each other to keep quiet, even if they themselves couldn't.

In the pale light Josh recognized them. A dozen guys from the team were carrying his Volkswagon Beetle to the space between the garage and the Tarzan tree. "He won't get it out for a month," one of them said, and stifled giggles rose to the open window. The group found the spot they wanted, and set the car down. They slapped each other on the back, gave a few high-fives, and then quickly ran down the driveway to the street. Now they were laughing with abandon. Josh heard the engines of several cars start and pull away.

The sound faded and the silence of the night returned. Josh looked down at his car. He looked at the gun in his lap. He looked at the car. He set the gun on the floor, and turned to look at the car again.

The tears began to flow. Josh spent the night in tears. He spent the night crying and looking at his car under the Tarzan tree.

⟜⟛⟝

William did not slur his words, and he spoke without hesitation. These were good signs. Much of his face was still covered in bandages, however, and his right eye was almost completely hidden under several layers of gauze which had to be changed four times a day.

But there was no mistaking the same calm, commanding voice. Alan would have recognized the voice even if he couldn't recognize the face. William was back. He acted like he wanted to get up and walk out of the hospital today. He had won the battle.

"How did you get up here?" William asked as he sat up higher in his bed.

"I brought Old Green," Alan answered. He was trying to be brave when he looked at William. "She's running pretty good, though I think the throw-out bearing in the clutch is going out." Alan paused. "The clutch is beginning to slip sometimes in the lower gears."

William smiled. He had had that old Dodge pick-up for over thirty years. He couldn't remember the number of hunting and fishing expeditions that machine had taken him faithfully to his destination. "When I get out," he said, "we'll take the clutch out and look at that bearing. You're probably right, though. Old Green hasn't been given my best care this year."

"How's everything at school?" William changed the subject. "You doing okay?"

Alan shook his head yes. "Fine," he answered. "The team is nervous about playing Garden Hill tomorrow, but other than that, we're doing fine."

"Don't think about it too much," William said softly. "The team has much to be proud of this year no matter what happens tomorrow night."

"I guess," Alan agreed, "but they're the defending state champions, and they have great players."

"So do we."

"Yeah, but these guys are the best in the state. We can't stand toe to toe with them. We're just average guys. They're like, heroes."

"I think you have the wrong definition of what it means to be a hero," William said. "The nurse who changes the bandages on my head and volunteers at the food bank on the weekends is a hero. The gal behind the counter who sold you gas this morning and helps support her parents with her paycheck is a hero. The father who works long hours so his kids can have clothes for school, the guy who installs mufflers during the day and goes to school at night, a man who picks up litter, they are all heroic in my view, and they are all around us."

Alan said nothing.

"A hero is someone who knows we're not here on earth just to please ourselves," William said. "A hero is someone who knows we're all the same and we all need each other. But most importantly, a hero acts. A hero sees what must be done to make the world better, and acts on it. Hitting a home run in the World Series is a spectacular event, but it is not heroic. Lending a helping hand to someone who is in trouble is."

Alan shook his head in agreement. "Then I guess I know some heroes," he said.

"The world is full of them," William said again.

Two nurses entered the room, and in a nice way, ordered Alan out. "You wouldn't want to be responsible for any infection would you?"

Alan shook William's hand. "The game is going to be on the radio tomorrow," he said.

"I'll be there for every play," William said and squeezed Alan's hand. "Don't worry about them, just do your best."

"The fun's just starting," Alan said with a smile.

Alan felt relieved when he left the hospital. Everything would be all right. William would be okay. In a week or two he would be back home. Alan almost passed the car sitting on the shoulder of the on-ramp to interstate 35 heading south out of Wichita. What did a stranger's flat tire have to do with him? But he did stop. The Florida tag and the two older black women sitting nervously in the front seat told him he should.

Twenty minutes later they were ready to go. When they tried to pay Alan for changing the tire, he would hear none of it. Then he and Old Green headed back to Karo.

Leonard turned off the evening news, picked up his pipe and reached into his pocket for his tobacco pouch. As usual, it wasn't there. He grit his teeth and shook his head slightly. "I swear," he said softly, "if I don't lose track of that thing every day." He picked up the morning newspaper off the couch and saw the edge of the pouch poking out from underneath the cushion. He retrieved the small leather pouch containing the black Cavendish and opened it as he walked outside to the porch.

He sat on the bench and began to fill his pipe. It was late October now and the evenings sometimes required a sweater. He debated for a moment with himself whether he would be able to sit outside without one, and decided he would eventually need it. He lit his pipe and went back inside. He found a sweater that didn't smell too bad, threw it on, and stepped back out on the porch.

Leonard stopped in his tracks. Elaine was standing at the bottom of the porch steps. "Hello, Leonard," she said as she lifted up a yellow envelope. "I was driving by and I thought I would just drop off the results of the Alexander assessment."

For a moment, Leonard was speechless. "Thanks," he said, still motionless. "I can get an early start on that tonight." He wondered if the gratitude he felt upon seeing her was visible. "It's really good to see you," he said sincerely. He finally stepped out of the doorway, walked down the steps, and let the screen door close behind him.

"I was just thinking of going on a walk," he said. "It's such a beautiful evening. Would you like to join me?"

"Sure," Elaine answered. "That would be nice."

Leonard took the packet from her and laid it on the porch railing. He marveled at the fact that he was so calm. His mind was not racing with a thousand things to say. He was not worried about what to do. He was just being himself. He was Leonard Davis going for an evening walk with a beautiful woman.

"I'm really glad you came," Leonard repeated.

"I thought we should talk," Elaine said without hesitation.

Leonard knew when to answer and when to keep silent. This was a time to wait. He quickly buttoned his sweater and pointed down the road leading south from town.

Let's go down Kaufman road," he suggested. "There's a chance we might see deer or turkey." This was one of his favorite walking paths. After five minutes, all traces of civilization disappeared into a winding, shadowy lane whose hillcrests gave spectacular and panoramic views of the sun setting on the prairie.

"I don't know where to start," Elaine finally said.

There was another long pause, but Leonard let it hang for the longest time. "Does it have to do with us?" he finally asked.

"Yes, about us," Elaine answered, "and other things."

They made their first turn onto a gravel road which began a gentle slope to an old iron bridge over Miller's creek, one of the few single lane bridges left in the county. There was another long pause.

"All of my life," Elaine finally began, "I've found compromise easy to do, but also very difficult." Leonard thought she sounded almost apologetic. "It's not that I always want my way, it's just that if I believe in something strongly, I am not willing to give in on it."

"That's one of your strengths," Leonard offered.

"But I'm thirty four years old," Elaine said without looking at him. "I don't know how much longer I can live this way without making some changes."

"Changes?" Leonard asked.

"Yes," Elaine said. "I could be content to live the rest of my life alone, but I would also like to have a husband and family."

"You would make a wonderful wife and mother," Leonard said as an automatic response. They were now walking across the middle of the old iron bridge. Turkey creek trickled slowly thirty feet below them. A breath of wind stirred.

Elaine stopped, and for the first time, turned to Leonard while she talked. "Colin has asked me to marry him," she said.

Leonard closed his eyes. In an instant he was standing at the bottom of the Grand Canyon in the dark. He lost all his senses. He couldn't hear the evening chorus of the locusts. He couldn't see the setting sun. His tongue suddenly tasted bitter and the air around him had a pungent smell. Every sense he had turned against him. "This is what life can be," his senses told him. "Life can be acrid and nauseous. Life can be a preview of hell. Welcome to your new life."

Leonard finally opened his eyes and looked directly at Elaine. Her eyes were searching his. Were they showing turmoil as well?

"What was your answer?" Leonard asked without wanting to know.

"I said I needed a couple of days to think about it," Elaine said as she turned and slowly began to walk again. Her eyes returned to the road below her.

Leonard didn't know how, but he got his legs to move. His senses slowly came back to him. He could hear the locusts droning their eternal song. The bitter taste in his mouth began to fade. He saw the cloudless horizon in the west. He walked alongside Elaine for the longest time without saying anything. He didn't know what to say. He didn't know what to do.

"Colin has a lot to offer," Elaine said as if she were trying to convince herself of her words. "He offers security. He would not mistreat me. He would give me freedom and stability at the same time," she continued.

"Sounds like a new car," Leonard said.

Elaine turned to Leonard and frowned, but continued. "He is young. He would be a doting father. I would never have to worry about providing for any children."

"Does he love you?" Leonard asked.

"I think so," Elaine answered sincerely. "He says he does, and everything he does says so as well."

"Do you love him?" Leonard couldn't believe he asked the question.

Elaine stopped and turned to face Leonard, but she could only look him in the eyes for a second before they returned to the gravel road. "I…he treats me well, and it feels good to be around him," she said softly and began walking again. "We have been dating for several months now," she continued, "and he is always attentive. He is always concerned about what I'm doing and where I am." She paused and turned to look at Leonard again. "If I don't love him now, I'm sure I could learn to love him."

They resumed the walk, and Leonard decided not to respond. The bridge was now completely out of sight as they made their way up a hill. The trees thinned when they reached the crest. This was where he and Linda would often pause and watch the sunset. On some evenings, Kansas would present them with the best sunsets in the world. The sky would blaze into twenty different shades of red, each changing by the minute; darker would become lighter and lighter darker in a constant, subtle, and remarkable dance.

"I thought it would be an easy proposal to accept," Elaine said staring at the setting sun. "It never crossed my mind that I would have second thoughts." She stopped walking and turned to Leonard. Her lower lip was quivering. "But you have confused me."

Without warning, Leonard pulled her to him and lowered his mouth to hers. For an instant he felt a push of resistance, and then, sudden submission. It was a hard, passionate kiss. For three years Leonard had not kissed a woman like this and he was lost in it. They were both lost in it.

"Don't marry him," Leonard said when it ended. He still held her close. Their lips remained inches apart as he searched her eyes. "I love you," he said. "Please believe me."

"I don't know what to do," Elaine said softly. "Life is so hard."

"Life is easy," Leonard responded, "all you have to do is lower your standards."

Elaine immediately recognized her own words and slowly pushed away. There was a look of confusion on her face. "See!" she said as she backed away. "This is why it is so hard. I had things figured out, and then you come along and act like you are saving me from a big mistake. You can't just waltz into my life and suddenly become someone I love."

"Why not?" Leonard asked. "Why can't I suddenly become someone you love?"

"Because you are changing the rules in the middle of the game," Elaine said. "I could do a lot worse that Colin, you know. You act like you are going to save me from an execution. Well, I don't need saving."

"Then why this?" Leonard countered. "Why come to see me? If you were so sure of your plan, why not just say "yes" and get married? I could read about the engagement in the paper like everyone else." Leonard shot the questions off in rapid fire.

"Because you may be right," Elaine suddenly whirled to face him. "There! Are you happy? I came to see you because you may be right." Tears began to from and make their way down her cheeks. "It might be a mistake to marry Colin. I may not love him. I may be settling. I don't know." Tears began to flow now. "I may love you."

Leonard took her in his arms. This time he just held her. How could he not have sensed the torment she was going through? He was asking her to jump off a moving train. He may be asking too much.

He kissed her forehead as she wept in his arms. "You're right," he said calmly. "You need time to think things through." He brushed the hair from her forehead and wiped a tear from her cheek. "I'm sorry for pushing you into a corner." He stepped back and took both of her hands in his. "Whatever you decide," he said softly, "I want you to know that over the past couple of months, in spite of myself, and after a hundred sleepless nights, I have learned one thing for sure. I do love you."

Elaine nodded her understanding through misty eyes. "That's what makes it so hard," she said. "I just don't know what to do." She wiped her eyes with her sleeve and began to walk again. They hardly talked during the last stretch of road, but they did see deer. A herd of seven bolted across the road in front of them. It was almost dark when they completed the circuit of Kaufman road. The town of Karo began to unfold before them like trees coming out of a fog, and before they knew it, they were standing in front of Leonard's porch.

"Will I see you again?" Leonard asked.

"I don't' know," Elaine said. She kissed Leonard on the cheek and took the keys out of her purse. "I don't know," she repeated as she slowly walked to the car.

Leonard waved as she drove away. "Take care of yourself," he said. There was nothing else to say. There was nothing he could do. He watched her drive away and stood there long after the headlights were gone before he made his way back into the house. That night he dreamed he was standing at the bottom of the Grand Canyon in the dark.

⸻

The four officials introduced themselves and gave Leonard the card with their names and positions on it. Leonard could use that card to complain to the K.S.H.S.A.A. about an official, or he could use it to recommend some of them to work the state playoff games which would begin the following weekend. Leonard had never complained about the zebras. To him they were part of the environment. They were like an uneven field or a windy day. Sometimes they were good, and sometimes they were bad, but they were the same for both teams. He took the card and put it in his pocket.

"Is everybody legally equipped?" the referee asked. "Anyone you want us to check?"

Leonard shook his head no.

"What about trick plays? You got anything we should be aware of that might catch us off guard?"

Again, Leonard shook his head no. The referee asked to see the game ball, so Leonard sent the manager to the bench to get it.

"We want you to know," the umpire said while they waited, "that we will do everything we can to keep the clock going. We want to reduce the carnage as much as you."

This time, Leonard shook his head in agreement. "I appreciate that," he said. "I just hope the other coach is a good, reasonable man."

The linesman grit his teeth at that. "I've done three of their games," he said instantly, "and I don't believe you can expect a break from him. He's run the score up in everyone of them. He wants to get as good a seed as possible in the playoffs and stats look good to the public, you know."

Leonard nodded again in a sad acknowledgement of how things are. The manager returned to the group with the ball and the officials examined it. They synchronized their watches with Leonard and headed over to the other sideline to follow the same routine.

Leonard scanned the bleachers, but didn't find what he was looking for. It was time to go into the locker room for the last time this season for the pre-game talk. He called his team together and led them back to the gym. They walked slowly and silently, robot-like from the field. Leonard couldn't remember the last time he felt so helpless.

⸻

The yellow school bus filled with cheerleaders and students rolled into the parking lot. It was followed by a line of cars. On the back door of the bus was a shoe-polish message. It read, STATE CHAMPS! The Garden Hill Hawks faithful had arrived for the game.

From their spot in the press box, radio announcers Stan Getty and Bob Fredricks could see the bus enter and commented about it to their listeners. Bob and Stan had been the radio voice of the Hawks for the past three years and planned to follow them all the way to the state championship game the Saturday after Thanksgiving.

"Welcome back to the Karo football stadium, such as it is" Stan said after the commercial break was over, "for tonight's contest between the Karo Eagles and the Garden Hill Hawks."

"It looks to be a mismatch," Bob said. "The Hawks are on another roll, and, as a matter of fact, are undefeated in 39 straight games. They don't look to have too much trouble from the Karo Eagles tonight."

"That's right, Bob. The Hawks have won three straight state championships and are the favorites to repeat again this year. They bring an 8-0 record into this game and hope to use it as a tune-up for the upcoming playoffs."

"The Eagles, on the other hand, snapped a fifty-two game losing streak this year. In fact, they have won four games, and that is something nobody could have predicted before the season began."

"It has been a good year for the Eagles," Stan added, "because they broke that streak and come into tonight's contest with a 4-4 record. But they themselves have another streak they would like to break tonight, a streak of 27 years."

"That's right, Bob. Even though Karo has been eliminated from the playoffs, they have something else to play for. It's been twenty-seven years since any Karo team has had a winning season. And if the reports we hear are true, this may be their last chance, because this may be the last game played by a Karo High School football team."

"You're right, Stan. Word around the area is that the school will close at the end of the year. We may be witnessing the last game ever played on this field."

"Well, be that as it may, let's take a look at the coaches. The Hawks are coached by Roger Klinger, who as everybody knows, played college ball at Texas-Arlington and was on the practice squad a few years for the Cowboys. I believe his career was cut short by a knee injury, wasn't it Bob?"

"Yes, I believe it was."

"His assistant coaches are Bill Johnson, Greg Atenborough, Phil Rusato, and Mike West."

"On the other side of the field, the Eagles are coached by Leonard Davis and assisted by William Roundtree."

"I understand that coach Roundtree is unable to be at the game today, something about a dog bite, so Coach Davis will be alone on the sideline."

"That's right," Bob said.

"Correct me if I'm wrong," Stan continued, but isn't coach Davis the school Librarian?"

"Yes."

"And coach Roundtree is the school janitor?"

"Yes."

There was a long pause.

"It's amazing they have won any games," Stan finished his thought.

"Well," Bob continued, "they do have one very good player. Jason Moeller, number 33 for the Eagles stands about six foot three and weighs in at about two-hundred and ten pounds. He has been talked about by several of the coaches around this area. Coach Klinger himself told me earlier this week that they had a great deal of respect for this Moeller kid, and he wished he could have him as a Hawk."

"But the Hawks have their share of good players as well," Stan said. "They are led by their all-state fullback and linebacker, Larry Sturgis." Stan couldn't hide the excitement in his voice. "And he is a glorious football player. He stands at six foot four, two-twenty, can bench press 400 pounds, leads the state in touchdowns and college coaches all over the country were drooling up til last weekend when he made his choice of where he would go next year."

"I was at the signing," Bob continued, "and there must have been a dozen television cameras there. The place was packed, and the media showered him with more attention than he had ever had before."

"He'd better get used to it," Stan quipped.

"Well, all the stands are full," Bob continued, "and there are fans standing along the entire sideline. The Hawks have brought a good following tonight, and it looks like most of Karo has turned out to see if their Eagles can pull out a miracle."

"It's not likely, Bob," Stan said.

"I agree," Bob said, "but the Karo football team does have a chance for a winning season, something they haven't had for twenty-seven years. And if it's true about the school closing, they would surely love to go out with a victory."

"You're right about that," Stan said. "I would bet that inside the Karo locker room there is pandemonium. They're probably screaming and yelling and bouncing off the walls."

There was not a sound to be heard as Leonard scanned the faces in the bleachers. He saw confusion, worry and fear. On most faces the fear was obvious, on others it lay just below the surface. Leonard wondered if they saw the same fear in him. He felt like a pitcher poured dry.

"You're about to go where people seldom go," Leonard said softly. "Poets and saints maybe go there quite a bit, but the rest of us don't. We try to avoid it." Leonard let out a quiet sigh. "You are about to venture into your own heart."

"And why is it people don't like to go there? Maybe they're afraid of what they will find. Maybe they're afraid of the questions they must ask. Who am I? Am I good? Am I good enough? But if we don't visit this place, we don't know ourselves like we should. Because in this place all the decorations are stripped away and there is no place to hide, no place to run."

"It can be a painful place to enter, so many choose not to go. Some people don't like the results, they can't face the truth. They might find that their heart is wrapped in a dollar bill. They may find that their soul is full of fear and ignorance. Maybe they find they are empty beings, and it's painful when they discover they don't believe in anything. Self-discovery is never easy, and rarely painless."

"But we are going there tonight, and we should think about what we can learn when we visit. We should think of the lessons we can learn when we ask the questions we fear to know. Me? Well, I've learned that no matter the consequences, those who are honest with themselves lead a better life. I've learned that I can keep going long after I thought I couldn't. I've learned that I can do something in an instant that I would regret for the rest of my life. I've learned that it is possible to overcome weaknesses, and I've learned that life is simply one test after another."

"The strange thing is, even though each of us is alone in this place, we will never be closer to each other than we are right now. We will never capture this moment again, and we will never forget it. At this moment we are so united we could forgive each other's sins, and God would approve."

Leonard paused for a moment. "There's nothing I can tell you about this season that you don't already know. We've had a good year. We can be proud of ourselves. We fought the good fight. We have grown to love and care for each other. We have learned to depend and sacrifice for each other. I could not be prouder of each of you or this team."

Leonard paused and took a deep breath. "It may not be fair," he continued, "but we must test ourselves one more time against the state champs. After all we've been through, how can I ask you to do that? How can I ask you to go out there one more time and face your fear? I can't. You must answer that question yourselves."

"And in the end, does it matter if we win or lose this game? Not at all. But you will remember your decision. You will remember for the rest of your life whether you searched deep inside yourself and decided to face your fear, or cower under it. You will remember your effort and you will look back on this day as one of your finest memories, or you will look back on this moment as one of surrender and regret."

Leonard spoke louder now. "Being fearless doesn't mean bungee jumping off a bridge or skiing down a glacier. That's just adrenaline. Living without fear means knowing who you are in your heart, keeping your conscience clear, speaking the truth, and doing the right thing even when it's hard to do."

"So when we walk out on that field, I hope you choose to try. I hope you choose to embrace the challenge. I hope you choose not to let fear rule your heart. Living in fear is not life, it is existence."

Leonard finished speaking with a clear, quiet voice. "Rudyard Kipling wrote something that summarizes it pretty well, I think. 'If you can meet with triumph and disaster and treat those two imposters just the same, yours is the earth and everything that's in it."

Leonard paused again and a slight smile came over his face. "So whatever we meet when we walk out that door, be it triumph or disaster, we will stare into the face of the imposter and know that we are greater than what awaits us. We have visited our heart, and we will stand tall, and we will stand proud."

Leonard suddenly realized he had been talking to himself, but it didn't matter. Every eye and every ear was on him. "I want to thank you," Leonard said as he wiped a tear from his eye. "You have given me so much joy this season, and I am a better man for having been a part of your team. Thank you," Leonard smiled sincerely. "I love you all," he finished and wiped another tear.

There was silence in the stands for a moment, and then Alan stood, holding his helmet under his arm. His face showed stone-cold determination. "Hahnah-Hahweha," he said simply. "We are one, we are strong." Brad rose next to him. Hahnah-Hahweha" he said. "We are one, we are strong." Josh and Jason rose together. "Hahnah-Hahweha," they said in unison. Greg and the rest of the team rose to their feet. Instantly they all rose to join in the chant. "Hahnah-Hahweha" the team chanted over and over to let the word know. "We are one, we are strong."

Leonard opened the door and led his team out toward the field. Be it triumph or disaster, they would face the imposter together, and not be moved.

Louis Freeman paid for his ticket and walked through the gate as he checked his watch. It was about five minutes before kickoff. He had plenty of time to get some popcorn, so he veered toward the concession stand. He had a weakness for popcorn. It didn't matter if he was at the movies, a ballgame, or the county fair, he had to try the corn.

He looked around and judged the crowd to be a little over a thousand. Out on the field, the band was playing the Star Spangled Banner, so Louis removed his hat and covered his heart with it. They sounded quite good, he thought, and when it was over, he applauded their performance. The line at the concession stand was short, so he was able to get his bag of popcorn quickly. The first bite was crunchy and flavorful. It was good to have a weakness.

It was a beautiful evening, and Louis found himself looking forward to the contest. He hadn't seen a high school game since his son graduated ten years ago. Why had he waited so long? He took another handful of popcorn and chided himself for his negligence.

"Mr. Freeman," came a call from behind him. "I didn't expect to see you here." It was the familiar voice of Christopher Edwards. Louis turned around and shook hands in greeting. "Chris," he said through crunching popcorn, "how are you?"

"I'm doing fine," Christopher said and turned to his side. "You remember my wife, Tiffany." Tiffany stood next to her husband with a frozen smile. They had come to the game to work the crowd. The Board of Education's referendum was this coming Monday and even though their straw poll showed their position was leading by ten to twelve points, it was always a good idea to press the flesh and get as many sheep in line as possible.

"It's good to see you again," Tiffany said automatically. Her frozen smile thawed considerably, as she shook Louis's hand.

"I guess I'm just a little surprised to see you here," Christopher regained his composure. "I recall penciling in next Saturday, the 8'th as our day to look over the site. But I guess…I suppose we could look over the property now."

Louis waved his hand and shook his head. "No," he said through a mouthful of popcorn. "I didn't come to see the property." He finished chewing and wiped his mouth with his handkerchief. "Excuse me," he said as he wiped his mouth again. "I didn't come to see the property. I came to see the people. If I'm going to have a plant in this town, I need to know the kind of people who will live and work here. A building can be any type, but the people must be a certain type."

"Well," Christopher said a little off guard, "I'm afraid the people of Karo are well behind the times. Most of them probably drive their tractors to church on Sunday." He smiled at his feeble joke.

"It wouldn't matter," Louis said, "as long as they were going to church." He took another bite.

Tiffany stepped in to aid her husband. "The people are decent, but a bit thick," she said. "We live here because the property taxes are so low, and we save a bundle over what a new house would cost if it were in Wichita. In fact, with the lower property taxes on this building complex, the savings would be significant for the company." She could get no reading from the quiet, black man eating handfuls of popcorn one after the other. "If you were to acquire it," she added finally.

Louis nodded that he understood and finished another bite of the corn. "My sister and mother came up from Florida last week for a visit," he said using the handkerchief again. "Their car had a flat on the 135 ramp yesterday." Louis took another handful of corn from the bag without putting it in his mouth. "They said a hundred cars passed them by before this young man stopped to help. He pushed the car out of danger, changed the tire, and got them on their way." Louis took another bite. "He wouldn't take money, and he didn't say much about himself except to say he was a senior at Karo High School."

Tiffany and Christopher looked at each other. What the hell was he talking about? Neither knew what to make of it, and so neither spoke. The silence was broken by the loudspeaker welcoming everyone to tonight's contest. The player introductions were being made.

"This is good corn," Louis said and looked over toward the concession stand. "I may have to get another."

The whistle blew and Greg sprinted down the field as fast as he could to cover the kick-off. Within a second, a Garden Hill blocker ran to meet him. Greg gave a fake in one direction and stepped the other way. The blocker swayed as he attempted his block and missed making full contact. Greg deflected the opponent with his left shoulder, and the Garden Hill player veered away like a missile slightly off course before falling to the ground. He was now just a blur in Greg's rear view mirror.

Greg could see it forming ahead of him as he continued to sprint down the field. Here came the wall. Three Garden Hill players had fallen back in a strategic retreat to form a wall together directly in front of the ball carrier. They were looking to attack and destroy anything that got in their way. Out of the corner of his eye, Greg noticed a like-colored jersey on his left about a step behind. A team mate was with him. The first one to the wall would have to take it on so the second would be free to tackle the ball carrier. Instantly Greg judged his team mate to have a better chance at the tackle. Greg would have to attack the wall.

He would have to take on all three at once. It was un-natural act, he suddenly thought, to run full speed toward three people who were running full speed toward you, and then with deliberate intention, collide with them to knock them down. His mind didn't quite see the logic in this.

Greg tried to get one more burst of speed before he coiled his legs and left his feet jumping towards the three. The first opponent tried to fend off the human projectile with his hands. The second had more of a warning and lowered his shoulder in an attempt to meet the flying man head on. The third member of the wall wasn't even looking at Greg. He had his sights set on someone else on his right. He had no idea his other two team mates were already engaged.

Greg flew into them at full speed. For an instant, they formed an airborne ball of arms and legs. The first two knew what was coming so when the collision occurred, they had protected themselves. The third was abruptly spun from his course, and twisting on one leg, tried to continue to run. But it didn't happen. All four of them fell in a heap with Greg rolling underneath all of them. The wall was down, and the ball carrier was defenseless against the upcoming tackle.

And what a tackle it was. Greg looked up from the pile of bodies just in time to see Jason headed on a clear path to the ball carrier. Like a guided missile dead on its target, Jason zeroed in. There was no escape. Jason stopped the Garden Hill player and drove him into the ground several steps backward from where they had met. A roar went up from the crowd.

Greg rolled off the ground and jogged toward the defensive huddle giving Jason a pat on the back. The game was twelve seconds old. One play down, a hundred more to go.

Josh cut outside the crashing end and barely kept his balance. The option wide would be there if he could get the pitch from Brad. He looked up quickly to see what the strong safety was doing. He couldn't see him. That could only mean one thing, the safety was rotating to the strong side. The weak side option was working well now that they had figured out the secondary rotation that Garden Hill was using. As a matter of fact, they had played these guys to a scoreless draw for the first quarter. Damn, it felt good!

Josh looked back at Brad just as the pitch came to him. But Josh wasn't ready. He should have been preparing his hands instead of looking down the field. "Catch the ball first," he scolded himself. Now it was too late. The ball hit him on the shoulder and bounced away from him. He tried to stop, but his feet slipped and he was suddenly lying on the ground as the ball rolled away from him. He scrambled to crawl over to it, but it was too late. That same Garden Hill end he had avoided earlier was scooping up the ball and heading down the field in the opposite direction.

Josh quickly sprang to his feet to give pursuit. He didn't see the blocker coming from his left side until he was once again on the ground flat on his back. Josh heard the roar of the crowd and lowered his head to the turf. What had he done? He had just given the other team a free touchdown. He slowly got up and walked to the end zone.

The Garden Hill players were celebrating. The ball was spiked and the scorer was beating his chest as he pointed to the heavens. His head was bobbing up and down as he began to wave his finger in front of him. "Don't bring that stuff my way," he shouted. Quickly he was surrounded by his fellow team mates, and they all swayed back and forth in a dance. When the celebration was over, they jogged back to their huddle for the conversion attempt.

One of them walked closely by Josh. "Loser," Josh heard as he trudged toward his team mates.

⊂⊃

"Nothing personal," Jason said as he lined head-up on the center, "but I'm going to kick your ass so hard, you're going to fart through your nose." The long-snapper looked at Jason warily. He had reason to be nervous. Everyone on the Garden Hill team had commented about how good number 33 on the Karo team was. He was easily the best player they had seen all year. As for Jason, he had never had a better game. In the back of his mind, he kept thinking that this might be the last game he ever played, so se wanted to remember it as his best.

The punter called the signal, and the center lowered his head to find the target. His first concern was to get the ball back there for a clean kick, so for the moment he ignored the guy directly across the ball from him. The snap was low and came to the punter at his ankles. The center sighed inwardly. He hoped there would still be time to get the kick away.

He hadn't counted on Jason bulling his way straight through the middle. True to his word, Jason crushed the center to the ground the instant he snapped the ball. The other blockers caved in to stop Jason, but had little effect. Jason had the perfect angle and his combination of strength and speed had him in the Garden Hill backfield before anyone could stop him.

Jason swatted the punt immediately after it left the foot of the kicker, and his momentum carried him forward where he lost his balance and stumbled. But quickly, he found himself near the ball which had bounced up towards him. He scooped it up and rumbled toward the end zone. A Garden Hill player attempted to tackle him, but only managed to be carried the last five yards for a score.

Jason jogged over to the official and handed him the ball. His team mates congratulated him, and then they all jogged back to their huddle. The two point conversion was good. The half was almost here and the game was tied 8-8.

Samantha turned up the volume on the radio. "Is that better?" she asked and William nodded yes. Samantha was happy to see him sitting up and moving. Most of the bandages had been taken off his head, but the ones on his legs and right shoulder were still there. There was a patch over his right eye. The doctors said only time would tell, but they had every reason to believe William would regain full sight. Samantha could see that William was getting stronger every day, and some on the staff were talking about releasing him within a week. William thought he was ready to go home now.

William settled into his pillows as Samantha sat down next to the bed. The commentators were simply gushing about the game. "I don't believe I have seen a better played half by both teams," one of the said, "at least on the high school level. Our stat sheets show exactly one penalty in the first half, a delay of game on Garden Hill in the first quarter. Stan, do you ever remember seeing a high school game with only one penalty in a half?"

"Can't say that I have," his partner answered. "But that's just an indication of the level of play we have seen here today. Both teams are extremely focused and the effort on both sides has been outstanding."

"Well, the defending champs find themselves in an unlikely position, tied at half time with a much weaker opponent."

"They may be much weaker on paper, but I've got to tell you, I was not expecting such an effort from the Karo Eagles. The way they are playing, it's not beyond the realm of possibility for them to pull the upset."

William turned the volume down and turned toward Samantha. "What we need to do," he moved his good arm as he talked, "is run the counter option. When they set up in their wide tackle six, we need to show option one way and come right back in the opposite direction. If those tackles flow like they are supposed to, we should be able to get to the outside. Especially to the weak side."

"William," Samantha called sternly, "you're puling the I.V. needle out of your arm."

William looked down. Sure enough, his gestures had pulled the tape away from his arm and the needle was loose.

"Now you settle down," Samantha chided as she came over and re-taped the needle.

"Yes, nurse."

Samantha leaned in and gave William a kiss. "You have every right to be excited," she said. "That's your team too. Those are your boys, and whatever happens at the end of the game is part yours as well." She gave him another kiss. "I'm very proud of you."

William looked for a long time into her eyes. "You are the best thing that ever happened to me," he said. "I love you." Samantha closed her eyes and rested her head on his chest. For a moment they just held each other quietly.

"But don't flop around like a fish," she ordered.

"Turn it back up," William demanded. "The second half is starting."

"I've got to say," Bob turned to his partner, "this Moeller kid is the real deal. He has been all over the field. He is as good as any player we've seen this year. Especially when you add Sturgis from Garden Hill to the mix. Those two have made this a terrific battle. It's just fun to watch."

"Not just Moeller," Stan continued the thought, "this whole Karo team has been playing above all expectations. A tie game at the end of the third quarter? I would never have believed it."

"Neither would I," Bob agreed. "I would have bet a thousand dollars this game would have been a blow out by now."

"Second down now," Stan said into the microphone, "and Karo has the ball on their own forty-one yard line."

Brad whirled around for the fake and put the ball in Jason's arms. He pulled it out again. They had been giving the Garden Hill team a steady diet of Jason running the ball, now they would use that to their advantage. Jason doubled over as if he were trying to hide the ball. If he could convince the defense that he was carrying it, he could draw their attention while Brad attempted a pass. Jason saw Brad retreat a few more steps and then stand tall to find his receiver. There was only light pressure, so perhaps they had fooled the Garden Hill players.

Brad didn't see the Garden Hill player come crashing in on a blitz, because he came from Brad's blind spot. Larry Sturgis, the all-state player had a clear shot at Brad and he didn't slow down. He unloaded on Brad just as the pass was thrown.

Jason saw the hit and even heard the crunch of the contact when Brad was smashed to the ground. He saw the ball fall to the ground about ten feet in front of Brad, so he quickly fell on it. Sturgis got up and did his victory dance while Brad lay writhing in pain.

Leonard rushed out on the field and helped Brad sit up. The E.M.T. sitting in the ambulance came out on the field and, after a thorough examination, helped Brad to the sideline. It was his shoulder. Brad probably had a broken collar bone. At the very least, it was separated. The medics wanted to take Brad to the hospital, but he refused to go until after the game was over. He had them pack it with ice. Brad stood on the sideline cheering on the team through stabs of pain.

“Mr. Stewart,” Riley turned around to see a gray-haired, black man extending his hand. “My name is Louis Freeman. I understand that you are principal of this school.”

“Good to meet you, Mr. Freuhof. Yes, I am. Are you enjoying the game?”

“My goodness, yes!” Louis answered. “I haven’t seen such a game played so well by two high school teams in a long time. I am particularly impressed with the intensity and determination of your boys even though they are clearly outmanned.”

“Thank you,” Riley said. “Unfortunately, this is probably the last game that a team from Karo will ever play.”

“That,” Mr. Freuhof put his hands on Riley’s shoulder, “is what I want to talk to you about.” The two of them slowly walked away from the crowd as they talked to each other.

Alan lined up for another pounding. For the entire game, his job had been to keep the Garden Hill blockers away from Jason. Alan knew if he did his job right, he would have no tackles, no personal statistics, and no newspaper would even show that he had played. But he had to protect Jason. Jason would get the tackles and the headlines because Alan had protected him throughout the game. Alan knew it and Alan accepted it. He was a hidden part of the machine.

But the plan was working. Because of Alan, Jason was having the game of his life, and the Garden Hill players knew it. They were increasingly frustrated that they were not able to get to their opponent's star player because some big, slow doofus kept getting in the way. They began to take their frustration out on Alan, sometimes double and triple teaming him. Each time they did, they hoped he had had enough and would call it quits or at least slack off. But he never did. He was always back for the next play, always doing his job, never saying a word, and making it possible for Jason to have great success. The big, dumb, son-of-a-bitch just didn't learn.

So Alan lined up again, and on the snap of the ball, exploded into the line to take out as many of the other players as he could. He would usually get a blocker from each side and occasionally a back would lead on him through the hole. This time, however, in addition to the double team, Garden Hill sent a pulling guard from the other side and a lead blocker from the backfield. There were four blockers on Alan this time. He gave it a good stand, but he was pounded into the ground.

But Jason was free, and he read the pulling guard heading to the opposite side. It was either a trap or a sweep. Jason immediately determined it was a sweep. He bolted through the gap left by the guard as they pounded on Alan and saw the ball carrier receiving the toss in the backfield. His instincts told him to pursue full speed, but his training told him to hesitate, to make sure he was right. He looked instantly at the split end coming back behind the line of scrimmage. "Tricky bastards," Jason thought. They were running a reverse.

Jason changed his pursuit angle and headed deeper into the backfield. Sure enough, the reverse was coming his way as the split-end took the hand-off and began sprinting against the flow. But Jason was waiting for him, and there was no place for the ball carrier to go. He couldn't outrun Jason, even though he tried. Jason caught him fifteen yards behind the line of scrimmage and unloaded on him.

The Garden Hill player, Jason, and the football all rolled to the ground. Jason had hit him so hard he had knocked the ball loose. The split end lay on the ground trying to catch his breath. Jason jumped up quickly to find the ball and saw it rolling around about five yards from him. With just a couple of quick steps, Jason scooped it up and headed toward the end zone. It was a carbon copy of the first touchdown as he rumbled across the goal-line and handed the ball to an official. Karo went for a two point conversion and failed. But they were ahead for the first time in the game. They led 14-8 with the fourth quarter winding down.

"That touchdown belongs to you," Jason said to Alan as he entered the huddle.

Josh fell behind the receiver. He had taken the bait on the inside cut and had to turn completely around when he saw his receiver fade back outside toward the sideline. It was a perfect throw as the quarterback lofted the ball toward the inside shoulder of the Garden Hill receiver, and he caught it in stride. Josh took a desperate leap toward the receiver's legs, but he only got air. The crowd roared as the Garden Hill player spiked the ball in the end zone and began beating his chest.

Josh laid his head back on the ground. He couldn't look. He had just given up the lead. With only a minute to go, Karo had been leading. Now Garden Hill would add six more, and if they scored on their conversion they would win 16-14. After the game everyone would say how proud they were. They would talk about how Karo had given a gallant effort, and the players had played the game of their lives. But Josh would know the truth. The truth was that he had given Garden Hill the first score when he had fumbled, and he was the one who just now gave them their second score when they threw a pass over his head. He would be the reason Karo had lost.

Josh got to his knee, unsnapped his helmet, and looked at the ground. He wondered if the team would be better off without him. Everyone was playing so well and so hard, and he was going to cost them the game. He couldn't look any of his team mates in the eye. How could he? He slowly stood and began to walk toward the end zone for the conversion try. He felt an arm on his shoulder and turned to see Jason walking beside him. Josh had to look away.

Jason patted Josh's shoulder again. "You know," he said between labored breaths, "when coach talked about facing the imposter and standing tall," he paused for more air, "I thought of you."

Josh was shocked. He suddenly stopped where he was. He was speechless as he looked incredulously at Jason. How could anyone see him that way?

"Come on," Jason began jogging to the end zone. There was a broad smile on his face as he turned back toward Josh. "Come on barf-breath," he said. "We still have a few minutes to play. Who knows what will happen." Then he quickly turned and sprinted off.

Josh stood for a second longer. If others had that much confidence in him, it was time to stand up and be a man. He buckled his helmet and ran to join his team.

"Loser!" he heard when he passed the Garden Hill huddle.

⊶

Leonard looked up at the clock. Time was running out. They would lose 16-14. Garden Hill made the two-point conversion on a pass, and after kicking off, held the Eagles to an eleven play drive where they gave the ball back on downs at the Hawk thirty yard line. Now Garden Hill was killing the clock with their victory formation, and Karo used their three time-outs after every play to force Garden Hill to punt. Leonard just used the last one.

Leonard was never very good at math, but a forty yard punt from the fifteen yard line with no return would leave his team with about fifty yards to score in one play. He didn't have a field goal kicker that would get anywhere close. The pros hardly ever tried a field goal from the fifty yard line. In fact, the only kicker he had was Josh, and he only did kickoffs. But Josh could kick the ball a long way. His kickoff almost always sailed into the opponent's end zone. If he could only score from a kickoff.

Suddenly the hair on the back of his neck stood on end. He glanced at the clock and saw seven seconds remaining. He called the official over and said something in his ear. The official nodded and went back on the field to confer with the other officials who were gathered around the ball waiting for the time-out to end.

"Jason," Leonard called out to the field. Jason jogged over to the sideline and Leonard quickly pulled him close. "What is it, coach? Punt block? Return right?" Leonard nodded no. "I want them to punt the ball,"

Leonard said. "Don't try to block it. Garden Hill is going to keep everyone in formation to prevent just an attempt." Jason took a drink from a water bottle and looked quizzically at his coach. "Now, whatever you do," Leonard continued, "do not return this punt."

Jason's eyes widened. "But coach, our only chance to win is if I can return this kick for a touchdown," he said.

"The odds of that are astronomical," Leonard said. "Trust me on this. There is another way. Trust me. All I want you to do is give a valid fair-catch signal and catch the ball before it hits the ground."

Jason looked at his coach like he had lost his mind. Granted, the odds of him returning this punt fifty yards for a touchdown in seven seconds were slim to none, but he was the only one who would have a chance, and he had to try.

Leonard saw the confusion on Jason's face again, but there was no time to explain. "Trust me," he said again. "I've got a plan."

That was all Jason needed to hear. He had come to respect and love this man, and what mattered was what his coach wanted him to do. "Sure thing, coach," he said as he snapped his helmet and headed back onto the field. "One fair catch coming up."

The snap was perfect, and the punt was a high spiral which came down right at the fifty yard line. Jason planted himself directly under it and raised his right arm for the fair catch signal. Even though there were two Garden Hill defenders surrounding him, he never moved. He caught the ball, and the official whistled a dead ball for the change of possession. There were two seconds remaining on the clock.

A confused hush came over the crowd. What the hell was going on? That punt return was their last hope of winning, and the stupid coach wasn't even going to give it a try? Now instead of Jason running in the open field, they were going to do what? A last second hail-Mary? Brad was out of the game and even he couldn't throw the ball fifty yards. Besides the odds of completing a fifty yard pass were less than a punt return. "Where the hell did you learn to coach?" came a familiar voice from the back of the stands.

"Kick-off team!" Leonard shouted. "Kick-off team right here," he shouted again as he waved them around him. "Josh, get your kick-off tee," he ordered and Josh ran to get it. The team stood around him looking confused but unafraid. In fact, Leonard thought they looked very calm. They had just fought the best team in the state to a near tie, and he couldn't be prouder of them. But now was not the time to express that. There was still work to do.

"We're going to free kick," Leonard announced as Josh came running back with the tee. "We're going to line up just like a kickoff, but we're not going to move. We'll get in our stance, but we won't budge. The only one who will move will be Josh. Josh will kick off like he always does with only two differences. First, nobody can move while he kicks the ball, and second, if he kicks it through the goalposts, we get three points."

All eyes went to Josh. "Three points?" Alan asked.

"Rule 14, section 3," Ilir said.

"It's our best chance to beat them," Leonard said.

There was a brief silence. "You know what coach," Brad said holding the ice pack on his shoulder, "we're gong to beat these guys with a fifty-year old play."

"Well," Jason said through a smile, "that would be perfect. I would say Karo is about fifty years behind the rest of the country."

"People are going to remember the last game of the Karo Eagles," Leonard said and put his hands in the middle of the group. Seventeen hands immediately came together. "Whatever happens on this last play," he said with a quiver in his voice, "always remember what you did today."

The whistle blew and the official waved both teams back on the field. Karo broke their huddle and ran quickly onto the field spreading out across it for a kickoff. Josh walked calmly to the middle of the field where Jason had caught the ball and set it on the tee.

Pandemonium ruled the stands. "What are they doing? They can't do that! What the hell's going on?" The official moved the protesting Garden Hill players back ten yards from the ball. They would not be allowed any attempt to block it. They could only watch. It was, as the official explained to them, a "free kick." The Garden Hill coach raved on the sideline until two of his assistants grabbed an arm each and pulled him off the field.

The murmur that had grown to a roar became hushed. The stands, the sidelines, and the players on both sides stood in eerie silence. Josh lined up the kick and walked back his usual fifteen steps. He suddenly felt alone, but it was not because all eyes were on him. He was back in the fifth grade kicking with Alan and Brad and Jason and Greg on a summer afternoon. They were all laughing and being young. He was kicking for fun. He was kicking for the joy of the game, and for that moment, Josh didn't even notice there was a game being played.

The whistle blew and the official lowered his arm. Josh approached the ball with increased speed. It was just him and the ball. When he kicked it, he didn't look up immediately, in fact he didn't look up at all. He waited and listened. It didn't matter anymore if it went through. It didn't matter if he missed. He was more than the kick of a ball. He was more than a win or a loss. He was much more.

William picked up the radio from the table and shook it in front of him. "Will you guys shut up!" he shouted.

Samantha came over to the bed and took the radio from her husband. "Shouting at the radio will not make them be quiet," she said calmly and pulled it gently from his hands. William sank quietly back in his pillow. He didn't like it, but he would have to hear more from Stan and Bob.

"Well the thirty-eight game win streak for the Hawks could end here," Bob said with undisguised excitement. "And I've got to tell you, Stan, it has been one heck of a game."

"You'll get no arguments here," Stan replied. "Both of these teams have a lot to be proud of. The game has been clean, hard fought, and exciting from the opening moments. Neither team should have to lose, but in one second, one of them will."

Bob agreed. "Well, both teams are set for the free kick, and there is almost silence in the stands. I don't remember seeing a team attempt a free kick in all my days of following high school football."

"Or at any level," Stan added. "I think you'd have to go way back in the archives to see what's unfolding here." Stan paused. "Josh Hunter is approaching the ball, and the kick is away."

Leonard held his breath when the ball was in flight, and didn't exhale until it cleared the crossbar. The officials raised both arms signaling the score. The eerie silence of a second before erupted into crescendos of cheers and shouts. The Karo players began to jump up and down. Leonard stood numb. There were no words. He made his way to the center of the field to shake hands with the Garden Hill coach, who sincerely, offered congratulations.

From then on everything was a blur. His team had scattered all over the field to be with family and friends. Several of the Garden Hill players came to offer congratulations. The crowd behind him shouted KARO! KARO! Leonard was grabbed and hugged and clapped on the back so many times he lost count. He slowly made his way to the center of the field to call his team together. He had to tell them how proud he was of them.

“These are the kind of people I want working in the new plant,” Louis Freeman turned to Riley. “Hard working, playing by the rules, and unfazed by obstacles.”

“I’m sure you could convince a lot of them to work for you,” Christopher Edwards said. “We just have to be sure we can acquire the property for a reasonable price after the school closes.”

Louis turned to see Christopher and Tiffany right behind him. His demeanor suddenly changed. “No,” Louis said. “I think we should build.”

“But, Mr. Freuhof,” Tiffany protested. “Just think of the money you’ll save. Think of the start-up costs. Think of the profit loss.”

Louis had heard enough. He whirled in a fury toward the two, and his voice turned cold. “Do you two think you are smarter than everybody else? Do you think for a moment I couldn’t figure out what was going on? There are only two things I have to say to you. First of all, you will not make any money off these people, and secondly,” for added emphasis he turned directly toward Chris, “I want you out of my office. I won’t have any duplicitous little weasel as my assistant. Come Monday, I’m going to transfer you to the motor pool.”

Tiffany and Christopher looked at each other. They didn’t know whether to laugh or cry. “Get out of my sight,” Louis barked, and they slowly trudged off bickering with each other. “I told you it wouldn’t work," Tiffany said as they faded away. "Twenty-five thousand dollars down the drain," was Chris's answer.

Mr. Freuhof brought his hands to his hips and looked directly at Riley. "When your board votes on Monday," he said, "there's something you need to tell them first." He brought his hands forward and folded them on his chest. "Two years from now there will be a plant producing the parts for our new airplane sitting right here in Karo. I'm going to recommend that we build the new production facility here when we meet with financial next week. And, since I'm the one who makes those decisions, I'm sure that my recommendation will be approved."

Riley was stunned for a second, but only for a second. "Two years from now," he said slowly. "Our school will double in size. If you build here...the population...the enrollment...the tax base...the school will be...

"Saved," Louis finished the sentence for Riley and extended his hand. "Congratulations," he said. "You should be very proud of your community, your school, and especially your students."

⊂═⊹ ⊹═⊃

William was jumping up and down in the bed. Samantha was on her feet whirling in circles. The radio announcers could not be heard over the din. Like a three year old child, William was trying to jump higher with each bounce from the bed. He was whooping and hollering. The I.V. tubes in his arms dangled uselessly from their patient. The poor hospital bed groaned and creaked with every jump, threatening to send its flying Walenda to the floor.

A nurse opened the door and her face of concern suddenly became dumbfounded. Instantaneously, a second and third nurse gathered with her, each with their mouth open and eyebrows up. "Mr. Roundtree!" they shouted almost in unison. "Mr. Roundtree! Stop that! What's going on? What are you doing?"

Upon seeing the nurses, Samantha went to the bed and pulled at William's gown to calm him down. Quickly, William stopped the bounding and stood quietly in the middle of the bed. He took Samantha's hand and looked at the trio of nurses as if to ask what the problem was.

"There's pudding tonight," William said to the three astonished, blank faces staring back at him.

“Be gracious,” Leonard said calmly to the team huddled around him on their knees in the middle of the field. “When you talk about this with others, don’t boast, be gracious. But most of all, be grateful for what you experienced today. Some people go their whole lives and never feel it. They know of it, and they long for it, but they have never experienced it. So tonight before you go to bed, hit your knees and thank the good Lord that you know what it is like, for one shining moment, to have put yourself to the test and be truly alive. I’m proud of every one of you. Go hit the showers.”

The team erupted with cheers from their circle and began heading toward the locker room. They did not scatter, but walked as a team toward the school. Leonard watched them as they congratulated each other as brothers. The season was over, and they would remember it. He hoped each one would wear it as a badge on his heart.

Leonard took Brad by the arm and began to lead him toward the ambulance, but an E.M.T. took his place and guided Brad toward the parking lot. “I’m glad you stayed,” Leonard said.

“Coach, I wouldn’t have missed it for the world,” Brad responded.

As the field was clearing, Leonard noticed a lone woman standing near the bench. She was looking at him. He nervously took a step in her direction. She did not move and continued to stare at him. There was a smile on her face. He lost her for a second as the team passed between them. Leonard suddenly found it difficult to breathe. Could it be? He dared not hope, but he did anyway as he walked slowly toward the lone figure. His heart leaped. It was Elaine. She watched him silently come to her. There was a wide smile on her face and a tear in each eye.

Leonard stopped at arm's length and swallowed hard. He couldn't speak. She was here. She had come back. Had she chosen him? His heart was full, yet he was at peace.

"Congratulations, coach. It was a wonderful game," Elaine said through her smile.

"What about Colin?" Leonard asked calmly.

"I told him no," Elaine paused and her smile broke into a tearful laugh. "I have higher standards."

Leonard rushed into her open arms and they were lost in an embrace. All around them people stopped, turned and applauded. Cheers went up from the team, and a new round of shouting was heard. But the two kissing on the forty yard line didn't hear them. They didn't hear a thing.

Frost covered most of the metal support of the bench. The pine slats, however, were frost free. Maybe, William thought, the iron gets cold faster, or holds the cold longer. More than likely, though, someone just got up from sleeping on that bench and their body had protected the wood from the frost. They were probably off looking for their breakfast and that first drink that goes with it. This park always hosted a dozen or so guests every night and William could see them beginning to stir out from under their blankets, newspapers, and boxes.

He saw a lone figure sleeping in a gazebo. He recognized a stocking cap with a Steelers logo, and began to gently shake the layers of coats covering the man lying on the bench. The movement slowly brought the man to awareness, and when he saw he was not in danger, the man began to sit up shedding several coats as he did. William smiled and took a deep breath. He had found Pinky.

The multi-layered creature rubbed his eyes and looked at the intruder. It took him a little while to focus his eyes, and another little bit to recognize the man standing before him. For a minute neither said anything. Pinky adjusted the top of the coat around his shoulders.

"Hi there, Chief," he finally said. "What happened to your eye?"

"It's a long story," William answered and took a seat on the bench. "Why don't I tell you about it over a hot plate of biscuits and gravy? I think," William said as he rubbed his chin, "I think I still owe you a meal."

"I believe you do," Pinky said as reached down to tie his bootlaces. "I believe you do," he repeated.

William led Pinky to "old green" and opened the passenger door for him. When they were both inside buckled and warm, William pulled out into the morning traffic. The clutch slipped again. "I'm going to have to get Alan and replace the throw-out bearing on this." William thought.

The rest of the pick-up worked fine. In fact, there was one addition William was especially proud of. He had a print shop make it for him last week. On the back bumper was a custom-made sticker saying I DON"T WORSHIP PETULANT CHILDREN.